Amity Hudson Edmonds has a past that she would like to forget.

Enid spoke gently. "Go on, Amity. Tell me about Chad."

Amity spread her fingers over her legs in a helpless gesture. "I was so eager to believe we were meant for each other that I ignored the signs. It's my fault. I suffered for it then. . . and I'm suffering for it now."

Enid's glance sharpened. "How?"

Amity hesitated, avoiding her aunt's eyes.

Enid reached over and tilted Amity's chin up. "Did he hurt you?"

Amity bit her lower lip to keep it from trembling. She nodded, still not looking at her aunt.

"He did! He really did!" Enid sprang to her feet and rammed her hands into the back pockets of her jeans, then she paced the floor with angry movements.

"The first time was three days after the wedding." Amity's voice shook.

Shirley

HANNAH ALEXANDER is the pen name for a husband and wife writing team from Missouri. Melvin and Cheryl are very active in their home church as well as in missions work in other countries like Russia.

The Healing Promise

Hannah Alexander

Heartsong Presents

I would like to thank the staff, actors and actresses, and administration at the Christ of the Ozarks in Eureka Springs, Arkansas, for allowing me to take part in the Great Passion Play. The experience encouraged, uplifted, and taught me what I needed to know to give this book authenticity. I also thank Dr. Melvin Hodde for his valuable medical input, and his plotting and editing expertise. Thanks, also, to Lorene Cook, my mother, for her constant encouragement and support. Freelance editor and writer, Barbara Warren, also deserves a great deal of thanks for all the hours she committed to ripping this work apart and helping me put it back together again.

A note from the author:
I love to hear from my readers! You may write to me at the following address:
Hannah Alexander
Author Relations
PO Box 719
Uhrichsville, OH 44683

ISBN 1-57748-320-0

THE HEALING PROMISE

Cover illustration by Kay Salem.

PRINTED IN THE U.S.A.

one

Amity Hudson gripped the steering wheel of her silver BMW so tightly her hands tingled, but she could not let go now, for the dangerous hairpin curves of Highway 62 curled like a snake down the steep mountainside. Dense, black clouds obscured the moon and stars, further darkening the night and making the road seem more tortuous still.

Shadowy trees, blowing in the wind, loomed over and around the car, threatening to engulf it and Amity into the deep green of the Ozark forest. The loneliness and silence jarred her fragile nerves and her imagination swiftly took hold. She shivered. Tiny hairs raised on her bare arms and her breathing quickened.

"Stop it!" she cried aloud, startling herself and dislodging the ugly visions of a pursuer from her mind's eye.

The reflection of headlights, growing ever brighter in the rearview mirror, heralded another traveler on the road behind her and she tightened her grip on the steering wheel. Her eyes strayed back and forth between road and mirror as the strange car eased up to a mere few feet from her rear bumper. She shivered again but breathed deeply and forced herself to remain calm. She loosened her tight grip on the wheel and squinted as she flipped the mirror to deflect the glare of the light.

It could be anyone, she knew that. No one was following her because no one even knew where she was going, not even Aunt Enid. . .yet.

The thought of Enid, her mother's practical younger sister, eased some of Amity's tension. Aunt Enid would take her in; Aunt Enid would know what to do.

Light reflected from the side-view mirror into Amity's

pensive, sea green eyes and she frowned. Why was that car following her so closely?

A pulse of harsher light streamed into her face when the driver behind her flashed his brights, signaling his intention to pass. Amity bit her lip and tasted the salty blood with the tip of her tongue as the car eased over into the other lane and pulled up beside her.

As both cars approached a blind curve, Amity's heart pounded in her ears as she saw headlights from an oncoming vehicle rounding the same curve.

Amity stomped on her brakes, squealing her tires on the pavement. Then she caught a fleeting glimpse of a scowling male face in the car beside her as he sped up and sliced in front of her, just in time to escape a collision.

Immediately after that, a pickup truck swept past and both automobiles disappeared into the night as a thin film of perspiration moistened Amity's upper lip. She raised a shaking hand and wiped her face. Did she know that man? She did not have a chance to see his license plate but what if he was from Oklahoma City!

She shook her head sharply. Since leaving home, every time a car had passed her she had panicked, but no one had pointed a gun in her face, as the anonymous caller had threatened to do.

As soon as she reached Aunt Enid's she would be able to relax, but how was she going to find her aunt's house? Last fall, when she and her folks were here, Dad had driven and Amity had paid little attention to the route that he had taken to get there.

Surely in a town the size of Eureka Springs, Aunt Enid's bed-and-breakfast, The Annalee, would not be that hard to find. But, in her rush to escape Oklahoma City, Amity had left her address book behind.

With a wry grimace, she glanced at the backseat of the car, which was crammed so full of her personal belongings that she could barely see out the rear window. In the trunk she had placed two suitcases full of as many of her dead husband's records as she could find.

Not that she felt she owed Chad's memory any loyalty after the way he had treated her, but someone was certainly searching for something in the house and Amity was determined they would not find whatever it was that Chad was supposed to have left behind.

As she approached town, the blackness of the night lifted gradually. Traffic grew heavier as a stream of cars emerged from the city limits of Eureka Springs, Arkansas. The flickering signs and the noise of motors and beeping horns served to dampen Amity's overactive imagination.

She sat back against the crushed velour of her seat and breathed deeply. Here were things she could deal with: traffic, congestion, and the raucous sounds of a busy metropolis. Not that Eureka Springs was a city, but lots of people wandered around, especially for this time of night. Some even walked alongside the road, at times visible, and at times blending with the shadows of the trees.

The road branched in a *Y*. Amity pressed the brakes again and stared at the signs in dismay. "Oh, no. Which way now?" The business route. . .Aunt Enid lived on 62B.

Amity sighed and waited for two more tourists to cross the street in front of her and then she turned to the right. But the curves did not straighten when she entered the residential section. In fact the road became more crooked and even narrower the farther she went. To make things worse, crowds of people still lingered on the roadsides, stepping out onto the street with little heed to oncoming cars. As she passed a small hospital, Amity wondered how many careless pedestrians visited there each week. With careful consideration, she eased on, stopping often for tourists and for cars coming from the other direction.

Four blocks farther along, she saw a sign up ahead. It was placed before a beautiful, obviously refurbished Victorian frame house. Amity squinted as she neared it. The sign announced: .

BED AND BREAKFAST
NO VACANCY

Just above the door frame of the house, another sign read:

THE VICTORIA

"Appropriate," Amity muttered, "but not what I want."

The congestion on the road gradually thinned, relieving her of the necessity of such intense concentration on driving but leaving her feeling more lost and alone than before.

Why hadn't she paid better attention on the way here last fall? Last fall, though, they had arrived in daylight.

A tall, heavyset woman waddled across the road in front of her car, and Amity rolled down her window. "Ma'am, excuse me, are you from around here?"

The woman stopped, turned around, and peered at her. Then she ambled up to the car, puffing heavily, as if she had just walked up one of the steep hills for which Eureka Springs is famous. "Why yes, hon. What's the matter? Are you lost?"

"Slightly," Amity admitted.

The woman continued to puff, leaning heavily on the car. "Hmph. That's just like saying you're 'slightly' out of gas."

Amity bit her lip. "Do you know where The Annalee is? My aunt lives there and I'm trying to find her."

"The Annalee. . .hmmm, let me see. . ." The woman rubbed her chin as she straightened from the car. A horn blared behind them and Amity jumped.

"Aw, hold your horses!" the woman shouted, then chuckled, waving the other car around. "Oh, yes, honey! You're talking about Enid Benjamin's place down the hill, aren't you?"

Amity leaned forward eagerly. "Yes, that's my aunt. Do you know her?"

"Sure do. We've been friends for years." The woman chuckled again, her eyes twinkling. "Her and her bright idea to change the name of her place, I almost didn't recognize it." She gestured along the road. "Just keep going the way you are. You'll pass the Crescent Hotel on your way. Now, that's a real interesting place if you have time to explore it later, but for now just follow this road right on past it and around a couple more curves and you'll be there. Enid just painted it fresh last year and now it's a real pretty light blue with navy blue trim. Can't miss it, 'cause it's one of the handsomest houses in town. You be careful now!" she called as Amity thanked her and drove on.

The homey, friendly attitude of the woman had served to ease some of Amity's tension and she now gazed with growing interest at her surroundings. Just as the woman had said, Amity had not driven far when her headlights illuminated a sign welcoming her to the Crescent Hotel. Through the trees, she caught a glimpse of a well-lit patio at the front of a huge, old stone building. Lights shone from several windows of the three-story hotel and people still meandered about the grounds.

As Amity turned left and followed the road down through a dark green tunnel of foliage, she made a quick mental note to return here later with her paints and easel. Last year she had not taken time to paint the Crescent.

Traveling in this direction, the buildings became sparser in number and just when Amity began to wonder if she were driving out of town, the road curved back on itself and passed more houses. One place, The Rosalee, caught her attention. She could just make out an outline of sculptured gingerbread molding that made the house look more like a fairy-tale castle. Last year Amity's mother had been enchanted by the place.

Still, it was not The Annalee and right now Amity wanted to find Aunt Enid to tell her everything that had happened and to hear Aunt Enid's voice reassuring her that everything would be all right. Mom and Dad would be upset upon learning that

Amity had told Aunt Enid and not them about this nightmare, but they had gone through a rough time last year with Dad's heart attack and they did not need more worries. Besides, they lived too close to the situation in Oklahoma City and Amity did not want to involve them in the danger.

Down in this section of town the street was quiet and Amity strained her eyes as she tried to get a good view of each house she passed. This was more familiar territory to her and one pretty house, a blue one, caught her attention. She tapped her brake. It was the Annalee! A sign, partially covered by foliage, stated:

THE ANNALEE, BUILT IN 1895
BED AND BREAKFAST
NO VACANCY

Amity sighed with relief as she guided the car alongside the curb across the street from the house and then stopped. Before turning off the ignition, she sat for a moment, gazing at the three-story house.

Trellises draped with honeysuckle surrounded the front porch and Amity breathed deeply the sweet scent drifting in through her open window. She read once more the sign announcing that there were no vacancies.

Although Amity had not warned her aunt that she was coming, Amity knew that she would be welcome. But would there be room? More importantly, would she endanger her aunt by staying here? Surely no one could find her here, but what if they did? What did they want and how far did they intend to go to get it?

But there was no other place for Amity to go and so she took a deep breath and squared her shoulders, then slipped out of the car, locking its doors before she left. After the long drive it felt good to stretch her legs and so she stood there, looking around for a moment, enjoying the refreshment of a cool breeze against her bare arms and face.

For an instant the clouds separated to reveal the huge, bright moon, flanked by several twinkling stars. But as she watched, the thick veil covered them again and the darkness closed in on her once more. She suppressed a shudder. Surely they could not get her here.

She ran across the street and up the flagstone sidewalk, taking care not to catch one of the slender heels of her shoes in a crack. She paused before climbing the shallow steps to the porch.

"May I help you?" a masculine voice drifted out to her from the shadow of trees.

She jumped back, her eyes flying wide open. "What?" She swung around, clutching her purse to her chest. "Wh–who are you?"

"Well, I'm not dangerous, I assure you," the deep voice replied with a tinge of amusement.

Amity frowned. That voice. . .

A tall shadow came forward into the dim light cast through the glass-paned door of the house. As the man approached the sidewalk, Amity took a step backward, for something about his movements was familiar. But then she caught sight of his mane of shoulder-length, wavy hair, and she realized she did not know him.

But tiny goosebumps prickled the back of her neck and she took another step backward, catching her heel on an uneven stone. She stumbled and cried out.

The man reached forward and righted her before she could plunge to the ground. He chuckled and then said, "If you're frightened, you only have to scream to bring everyone within a square block running."

She gasped. This time there was no doubt. "Titus?" she asked.

The man froze in place for a moment, then released her arm. "Amity?" His suddenly strained voice betrayed shock.

"Titus King, it is you! Oh, how wonderful!" Impulsively,

she reached forward to hug him, surprised by the wash of joy she felt at seeing him after the fiasco last autumn.

He stiffened and Amity released him, remembering how shy and ill at ease he had been with her last year until they had become more acquainted during her three-week stay.

"Amity?" He reached forward as if to touch her arm, then drew back. "What are you doing here? Is something wrong?"

She expelled a sigh. "I'm here for my health. . .to preserve it, that is. And something is definitely wrong." What a relief it was to know there would be someone else here she could trust, although the situation might be a tad awkward, considering the misunderstandings last fall.

"Is Aunt Enid here?" she asked. "Are you still staying here?"

"Yes and yes," he said as he stepped aside and motioned for her to precede him up the porch steps. "What's going on? Are you okay?"

"I'll tell both you and Aunt Enid about it at the same time. Where is she?"

"Right inside," he said and then rushed forward to open the door.

Light shone through the window of the front door, illuminating his face, and Amity stifled a gasp. His wavy hair, a shade darker than her own chocolate-brown hair, not only generously covered his head, but his face as well, in a fully grown beard and mustache. But those familiar sea green eyes, the same color as her own, looked out at her.

She brushed past his broad, muscular shoulders and stepped inside. At five feet, eight inches she was tall for a woman, but Titus dwarfed her with no difficulty. In her state of mind, if she had not known him, she would have been frightened of him.

A door opened down the hall and Amity glanced up to see her Aunt Enid step into it. The slender, black-haired woman looked at her, then squealed with delight.

"Amity! You really are here!" She rushed forward with outstretched arms and gathered her niece in a warm embrace. "When the call came asking for you, I thought they were crazy! Why didn't you tell me you were coming?"

Amity stiffened in her aunt's arms, then she pulled back and searched the woman's face. "What call?"

Aunt Enid frowned. "Why, a call came for you just a couple of hours ago. It wasn't your folks, and when I asked who it was, they hung up."

Amity felt as if she had been punched in the stomach. Her ears began to ring and the walls spun crazily around her. As her body went numb, she felt herself falling but strong arms caught her as Enid cried out her name.

Nightmare images floated behind her lids, images of her husband's angry expression, his raised fist and, once again, she heard his threats about revenge if she ever left him. Voices, heard as if from far away, chased away the figures, chased away the image of her husband, until a splash of water trickled down Amity's face and neck. She opened her eyes to find Aunt Enid's worried face close to hers.

Amity struggled to sit up on the sofa where they had laid her. "Wh–what happened?" She absently wiped the water from her neck. "I didn't—"

"Faint? You certainly did!" Aunt Enid exclaimed, dabbing a moist washcloth at Amity's face. "Start talking, kiddo. Are you ill?" she asked as she traced the dark shadows under Amity's eyes with a gentle finger. "You look it. And you've lost weight." Her hazel eyes darkened with worry. "Honey, what's wrong?"

Tears of weakness and fatigue sprang to Amity's eyes, and she closed her lids, lying back against the soft cushions of the sofa. "It's a long story. I'll tell you in a minute. I. . .I really am tired. . ."

When she opened her eyes, it was to find Titus, entering the room with a glass of orange juice. He set it on the coffee table beside Amity.

Enid picked it up. "Thanks, Titus. Here, Amity, drink this, then start talking."

Amity obeyed her aunt's command and sipped the sweet juice.

Titus nodded to Amity, not taking his eyes from her face as he folded his long frame into the chair beside the sofa. "I'm sorry. I'm afraid part of this is my fault. I leaped out of the bushes and scared you half to death."

Amity took another sip of her juice and felt her strength returning. "It wasn't your fault, believe me. Besides, you saved me from flattening my nose on the sidewalk."

He fixed her with a hazy green stare. "Then why did you faint?"

Amity sat up, and as she did so the front door burst open and someone rang for service.

Amity paled. Her hands trembled and she had to set the glass down.

"Titus," Enid said, "would you please see to whoever that is? I want to stay with Amity and find out what's going on."

With a nod, he stood and walked out of the room, pulling the tall doors closed behind him. Amity could hear his deep voice as he spoke with someone in the outer hall, and she looked at her aunt apologetically.

"Sorry, Aunt Enid. I didn't mean to cause so much trouble."

Enid hurried to the sofa and hugged Amity close. Amity's throat tightened with tears again, and she clung to her aunt. "Enid, I'm so scared."

"Why? What is it? What's frightening you?" Enid released Amity and sat back, her dark-fringed eyes creased in a worried frown. "Why didn't you tell me you were coming?"

"I'm sorry, I should have called, I know, but I was afraid to use the phone." Amity laid her head back and groaned. "I left Oklahoma City in such a rush, and I still didn't escape them."

Enid leaned forward. "Escape who?"

"I. . .I don't know. I think it has something to do with Chad's death. Someone keeps calling me, asking me what I know."

"About what?"

Amity sighed and sat forward, crossing her arms over her stomach in a self-protective gesture. "I think Chad was. . . involved in something he shouldn't have been. But I don't know. He didn't exactly include me in his life."

Enid raised an expressive dark brow. "Meaning. . . ?"

"Meaning that for the three months we were married, we might just as well have been strangers. . .almost. He didn't talk to me about his business affairs. . .he didn't include me in his social life." She shook her head. "I don't even know why he married me, except he thought he might have access to family money."

"Lots of people have married for less. Everyone in Oklahoma City knew you were an heiress and an only child."

"I know, but please don't say you told me so. No one knows better than I do that I should have gotten to know him better."

Enid moved to the chair Titus had left and sat down. "I won't argue with you there."

Amity spread her hands. "But there's this wild, impetuous thing called passion, that I was blind enough to call love. In other words, I let the man 'sweep me off my feet.' " She pulled herself upright and leaned forward. "Aunt Enid, he told me he was a Christian and I wanted to believe him so badly that I overlooked a lot of things."

"Such as. . . ?"

"Such as the fact that he never discussed his faith with me. He always seemed to be conducting business or out of town, too busy to attend any worship services. And when I tried to discuss the Bible with him or talk about the things of God, he changed the subject as quickly as possible. I just didn't see it for what it really was."

"It happens," Enid said. "It's easy to let that happen when you want something so badly."

Amity shivered. "I was rebelling, too. Mom and Dad fell in

love with Titus when we were here last fall. They decided he was perfect for me and they pushed our friendship so hard it grew uncomfortable. Did you know Titus wrote to me and called me after we went back to Oklahoma City?"

"Yes, I knew," Enid said quietly. "You wrote back for a while, too. I saw your letters."

"Until I started seeing Chad back home."

"I know that, too."

"I shouldn't have abandoned the friendship, just because of Chad," Amity admitted.

"If you hadn't, Titus would have," her aunt responded. "I don't think he considered it just a friendship."

Amity grimaced. "You couldn't have proven it by me. Titus never even tried to get romantic. He never kissed me, never held my hand. On his way to Texas to visit his parents, he came by to see me in Oklahoma City and even then, though he went out of his way to see me, it was as if we were just buddies."

"Of course. Titus is the kind of romantic who believes in building a good, solid friendship before building any other kind of relationship."

"Last year, I didn't understand the concept, Aunt Enid. Now I do. Wish I hadn't had to learn the hard way." Amity gazed around the room, more to rest her thoughts than out of real interest. The room had been decorated with comfort in mind, with padded, late-Victorian pieces of furniture set in an attractive arrangement and lacy white curtains on tall windows. It was a restful place and its normalcy and old-fashioned charm made it easier to believe that she was safe. If only it were true.

Enid spoke gently. "Go on, Amity. Tell me about Chad."

Amity spread her fingers over her legs in a helpless gesture. "I was so eager to believe we were meant for each other that I ignored the signs. It's my fault. I suffered for it then. . .and I'm suffering for it now."

Enid's glance sharpened. "How?"

Amity hesitated, avoiding her aunt's eyes.

Enid reached over and tilted Amity's chin up. "Did he hurt you?"

Amity bit her lower lip to keep it from trembling. She nodded, still not looking at her aunt.

"He did! He really did!" Enid sprang to her feet and rammed her hands into the back pockets of her jeans, then paced the floor with angry movements.

"The first time was three days after the wedding." Amity's voice shook. "He told me the business needed help and suggested I borrow some money from Dad. I refused." She hesitated and spread her hands. "I guess he thought he could convince me. He didn't."

"Why didn't you leave the jerk? Why didn't you tell your folks?"

"Pride. They didn't like Chad and they'd tried to talk me out of getting married so quickly. Also, I didn't want them to worry."

"Couldn't you have told me? I can't believe you let that monster. . . !" Fury surged through Enid's voice. She wheeled and continued pacing. "What did he do?"

Amity hugged her knees to her chest and took a deep breath. "He was an alcoholic. When he drank, he started arguments, then slapped me if I disagreed or tried to ignore him."

"And you let him? Why, that. . . If he were alive, I'd have had him thrown in jail."

"He ridiculed me because of my Christianity, telling me I was a hypocrite because I wasn't as meek and subservient as the Bible said I should be."

Enid wheeled back toward Amity. "Why did you stay with that creep?"

"He threatened me. He said he had friends who would make it hard for me if I left him." Amity rubbed her eyes and leaned forward, elbows on her knees. "Besides, he was that way only when he drank."

"So he got drunk three days after your wedding? What a loving husband."

"I guess I kept thinking he would change. I prayed about it and I believed I should stay. That lasted only three months."

The door opened and Titus came back in. He glanced from Enid to Amity and closed the door behind him. "Is our patient feeling better?"

Amity nodded. "Much better, thanks." She glanced at her aunt then she fell silent.

Enid ran a hand through her curly black locks. "Titus, please sit down. Amity and I have a problem we need your help with."

Briefly, she related to Titus what Amity had told her so far, including Chad's alcoholism and cruelty to Amity, while Amity grew increasingly uncomfortable. Pride again. But, if she had concentrated on building her friendship with Titus instead of dating a charming, attractive, seductive weakling, she would not be in this position. She had brought all this on herself.

"He threatened her," Enid concluded to Titus, who had sat down beside Amity on the sofa, listening, with his lips drawn into a grim line, his eyes growing colder with each word Enid said. "He told her his friends would make it rough on her if she left."

Titus leaned back and stretched an arm along the high back of the sofa. "Chad died a little over a month ago, right?"

"Six weeks ago yesterday," Amity replied.

"Drowned in Lake Hefner?"

"Yes," Amity said, shivering.

"They said it was a suicide?" Titus asked gently. "I was here when your folks called to tell Enid. I was so sorry to hear what you were going through."

"Thanks, Titus. Yes, the official report was suicide. But I have reason to believe differently."

Titus raised a brow. "You mean an accident?"

"I mean murder," Amity replied.

two

An antique clock ticked loudly in the otherwise silent room as Amity stared into the empty fireplace. Fear washed back over her. It was still too close and too real. And now someone had phoned her here.

"You don't believe he could have committed suicide?" Titus asked.

"Chad never talked about suicide. He wasn't the type. He never blamed himself for anything. He usually blamed me." Amity shivered and hugged herself, remembering.

"Tell me about his friends," Titus suggested. "What kinds of people did he associate with? What about his family?"

Amity shook her head. "His parents are dead. He has an uncle who is running for state office. His sister, Farris, lives in Oklahoma City, but I saw her only a few times after Chad and I were married. She came by to see me once since the funeral. It was not a friendly meeting."

Titus stiffened. "Farris? Farris Edmonds?"

"Why. . .yes." Amity turned to stare at him. "How did you know?"

"She was just here."

Amity's mouth went dry; she shook her head slowly. "That's impossible. I didn't tell anyone where I was going. I don't think I even knew myself until I was halfway here."

"Does she have short black hair, spiky bangs, blue eyes?" he asked.

Amity nodded, mystified. "What did she say?"

"She tried to rent a room."

Enid shook her head. "Amity, what did that man get you into?"

"You must have told someone you were coming here," Titus insisted. "Maybe you left a note lying around, or a map. And why would your sister-in-law follow you here?"

Amity looked at them helplessly. "I don't know. What worries me is that if she found me, someone else could, too."

"What worries me is your sister-in-law," Enid said.

"Chad inherited a lot of money from his parents," Amity said, "which was kept in a trust he could not break. He received a generous monthly stipend, which in Chad's opinion barely covered living expenses. Thus the need for more funds. Farris felt she should have received Chad's share of the trust after he died. In fact, he had made out a will stipulating that his money should go to her in the event of my death."

Enid gasped. "Could she be making the threatening calls to your home, too?"

Amity shook her head. "The voice was deep, probably a man's. Besides, Farris is openly antagonistic and she lacks subtlety. She wouldn't be able to resist identifying herself."

"Why didn't you come here when the calls started?" Titus demanded.

"You know how some people act after reading about a suicide in the paper. I figured it was just some weird crank caller."

Enid took Amity's hand and squeezed it firmly. "Tell us what he said."

Amity frowned, narrowing her eyes thoughtfully. "Something about. . .I don't know. . .he said if I went to the police, I would die the same way Chad did." She covered her face with her hands. "It's so hard to think about. It brings it all so close."

"Why would you go to the police?" Titus asked.

"That's the whole problem, I don't know. They said something once about a confession."

"A confession?" Enid asked.

Amity spread her hands. "Chad was apparently supposed to have made a confession, but I don't even know what he would have confessed." She shook her head. "Maybe I don't want to know."

"You need to know," Titus said. "What frightened you badly enough today for you to leave the city?"

"Someone ransacked my house." Amity hugged her knees to her chest. "I came in from grocery shopping and found everything scattered around all over the house, upstairs and down."

"Did they take anything?" Enid asked.

"Nothing that I could tell. All of Chad's personal and old business records were locked up in a safe in the attic and they didn't find it. I've been meaning to go through them, but I just haven't had the time. There's so much of it. Maybe I've been subconsciously putting it off."

"That's ridiculous," Enid snapped. "The more you know, the safer you'll be. Where are those records now?"

"Out in the trunk of my car."

Titus stood up. "Give me the keys and I'll unload the car. Then I'm going to call the police."

"No!" Amity sprang up from the sofa. "Not the police! I told you the caller warned me about that. He said he had access to the police computers, and he would know the minute I contacted them. I don't want to take the chance that it's not a bluff."

"She may be right," Enid said. "We don't know how dangerous it would be."

Titus expelled an impatient breath. "You can't expect to handle this yourself. You need help and the police can offer you protection."

Amity dug her car keys out of her trousers pocket and handed them to Titus. "No. Please. I know you mean well, but please don't call the police. What could they do right now? I wouldn't know what to tell them, except about the crank calls and the ransacking. That's not enough to do any good. They'll think I'm just some scatterbrained female who's overreacting."

Titus took the keys. "Then you need to look through Chad's records to see if you can find out something that will do you some good. I'll help, if you want."

"I know you're right," Amity said. "The more I know, the more advantage I'll have over these creeps who keep calling me. I can only pray that they don't know where I am, that they didn't follow me. . .or Farris."

Enid stood up. "Honey, that sister is too close for comfort, in my opinion. Everything points to her."

Amity shook her head. "I know how it looks, but I can't bring myself to believe that. She and Chad weren't very friendly with each other. The only thing she could have against me is the fact that I inherited the money she felt was for her. I don't see any reason why she would be making the crank calls. Or having them made by some man."

"It could be a petty way of getting back at you," Enid suggested. "If she believes it's a suicide, maybe she blames you. Or maybe she's just trying to scare you, or—"

"Or maybe she really does want to hurt me, to see me dead so she can claim the rest of the inheritance?" Amity shook her head. "I really don't think so."

"You said yourself that you'd seen her only a few times," Enid said. "How can you know what she's like?"

Titus jingled the keys. "I'll go empty the car while you two argue. Let me know what you decide." He pulled open the double doors of the sitting room and strode out into the hall.

Amity watched him leave, then turned back to her aunt. "I don't know what to think, Aunt Enid. Maybe Chad's papers will tell us something. But please," she said, reaching out to touch her aunt's slender, tanned arm, "don't tell anyone else about this. The fewer who know, the safer I'll feel for now."

Enid took Amity's hands in her own. "Okay, sweetheart, I won't tell anyone else for now. But I'm sure glad Titus knows. If you really are in danger, there's no one else I would trust more than Titus."

"I know. I'm glad he's here." Amity turned away and walked toward the long front windows of the room. She watched as Titus stepped out and walked down the sidewalk, across the street, and unlocked her car. "Let's just hope I'm jumping to conclusions," she said. "Maybe the danger is only in my imagination."

"That's fine, but don't let down your guard," Enid said. "Sometimes fear is a good thing."

Titus was still out at the car when the sound of heavy footsteps reached the two of them. A light tap at the sitting room door sent Amity's heart pounding with fearful anticipation. She froze as she watched her aunt stride quickly to answer the summons.

Enid barely cracked open the door at first. Then, "Clem!" she exclaimed, throwing the door open wide, her cheeks flushing to an attractive shade of pink. "What brings you here this time of night?"

Lifting one expressive brow, Amity forgot some of her fear as she looked over this newcomer. He was obviously a friend of Aunt Enid's. . .more than a friend, from the looks of it. Amity's gaze traveled from a head of coal-black hair, frosted with white at the temples, to a tanned face, to dark brown eyes that glowed with warmth as his gaze rested on Enid. He looked about forty-five. And, at the moment, he had eyes only for Enid.

"You, dear," he said, "you bring me here. I thought you were going to meet me after the play." His tone was faintly accusing and Amity regarded her aunt with growing interest. It was a welcome diversion.

"Oh. . .well. . .something came up," Enid stuttered. "Come over and meet my niece." She turned from him. "Clem Elliot, this is Amity Ed—"

"Amity Hudson," Amity interrupted. Ignoring her aunt's surprised expression at the use of her maiden name, Amity stepped forward and extended her hand. "I'm sorry, I'm afraid it's my fault Aunt Enid missed her appointment with you. I showed up on her doorstep without warning. If you'll excuse me now, I'll go see if Titus has my car unloaded yet." She smiled at her aunt, walked out the doorway, and closed the doors behind her.

So, her attractive, vibrant, forty-year-old aunt had been touched by the tentacles of love at last. And was struggling against it with every part of her, Amity mused wryly. "And now I've come and dumped this on her," she muttered to herself.

She met Titus as he carried in a load of her clothing. "You don't believe in suitcases, do you?" he said dryly as he handed her the keys and started up the stairs.

"Chad's papers are in the two suitcases I have. Where are you taking everything?"

"Follow me and I'll show you."

She stepped up after him, running her hands along the polished mahogany stair rail. Her feet sank without sound into the deep mauve, sculptured shag carpet as she rushed after Titus. They did not stop on the next landing but climbed to the third floor.

Amity caught up with Titus as he passed beneath a hanging lamp of milk glass and brass. Ornate mirrors and a raspberry-colored, overstuffed bench decorated a tiny alcove, into which Titus stepped. He swung open a tall door and stood back for Amity to enter.

"Is this Aunt Enid's room?" she asked, stepping into a beautifully appointed apartment.

"Yes, it is. I imagine you'll be staying here until another bedroom becomes available."

The walls were painted a discreet off-white, an excellent background for the pretty, sometimes ornate pieces that Enid had used to decorate. Amity especially liked an oak whatnot shelf placed next to the window and set tastefully with delicate figurines of women with umbrellas, horses pulling carriages, and gentlemen bowing. All was new since Amity was here last.

The carved wooden chairs, footstools, and especially the bed, with its cherry and maple wood, all blended together pleasantly. Amity stepped across to a mahogany washstand, complete with floral-painted pitcher and bowl, immersing herself in the atmosphere and pushing from her mind the outside world, a habit she had practiced a lot since things started going so badly with Chad.

"Does Aunt Enid use this or does she have a bathroom up here, too?" she asked.

Titus laid his burden down on the queen-sized bed covered by a wedding ring quilt, and opened another door. "Don't worry. This apartment comes complete with bathroom and extra bed." He tugged at a lever and pulled out a twin bed from the wall. "And if you're wondering how I've come to be so intimate with this room, it's because I helped with the carpentry work when Enid decided to fix up the third floor."

Amity walked over to the corner where he had placed her things and she picked up some of her blouses. "You do good work. I'd never have known a college professor would be able to handle carpentry tools the way you do."

"Thanks. Why don't we glance through some of Chad's files tonight? The sooner we get started, the sooner we'll know if you have anything to go on."

Amity hesitated. "I guess we could. I didn't have anything to do with his business and he never talked about it around me. He was an independent accountant, a CPA, and his business partner and secretary took care of his books after. . .after he died."

"If this is going to upset you too much, I can go through it myself," Titus said. Concerned for her, he surveyed her face. "You've been through a lot the past few weeks."

"It's been confusing. . .disturbing." Who was she trying to kid? It had been horrifying and Titus's expression told her he knew that. "I think, aside from the fear of the calls and the ransacking, the guilt I felt over his death has been the most upsetting."

"Guilt?"

She sat down on the bed. "It was like Aunt Enid said, we weren't happily married. I guess I felt guilty because I didn't mourn as deeply as I thought I should have." She stared, unseeing, out the window. Her grief process had begun long before his death, when she had discovered that the man she thought he was had never existed. "I keep wondering what happened to his soul. He was not a Christian." It was a statement of understanding, not a question. "I should have realized that before it was too late," she said. "How can you know the truth about a person when he says he's a Christian then lives like the devil?"

"You shouldn't let guilt eat you up. You did your best, judging by what you've said, and anything more than that was his own responsibility."

"I blew it big-time, Titus. I married the wrong man." She glanced at him. He did not meet her gaze but a telltale flush stained his neck. Maybe Aunt Enid was right. Maybe Titus had been more serious about her than she had thought.

"I relied on shallow physical attraction and thought it was love," Amity said.

"Um, you don't have to tell me this." Titus shifted uneasily on his feet. "I'll go get the rest of your stuff."

"Sorry, I don't want to embarrass you. It's just that I feet as if you and I became good friends last fall and that I could tell you a lot of things I couldn't tell many other people."

Titus glanced at her, then away. "You never mentioned much about Chad in your letters to me." The flush deepened, what little she could see around the beard.

"No, I didn't. Maybe I thought you'd disapprove, just like my parents did." She sighed and spread her hands. "Look, I'm a grown woman, twenty-six years old, but I obviously have a lot to learn about life. My marriage to Chad was probably one part infatuation, one part rebellion. It was eight parts stupidity. I let myself, you, and everyone else down."

"You didn't owe me anything."

"I owed you better treatment than you received last year. You were very kind to me and when Chad came along, I just—"

Titus reached over and took the keys from her hand. "I'll be back with the suitcases in a moment."

"Don't bother tonight," Amity said. "I can't bring myself to look through them right now."

"Then I'll do it. I'll take both cases to my room and look through them tonight. If I find anything, I'll let you know about it in the morning."

Amity cast him a grateful glance. "You don't have to get involved in this mess, you know. It isn't your problem."

Titus shook his shaggy hair back out of his face and grinned. "Do I look like the kind of man who would pass up the excitement of a mystery?"

Amity returned his grin. "No. Speaking of looks, what's with all the hair? You didn't even have a mustache last fall, and your hair was barely over your ears."

He walked to the door. "This past year I took a sabbatical from teaching college students. I became the Apostle Peter at the Christ of the Ozarks Passion Play. I wanted to look the part."

"Great! I'll have to come see you in it."

"You're welcome anytime. I'll get you a special seat." He smiled and his eyes held all the warmth she remembered. Kindness. Goodness. "See you in the morning," he said.

She smiled at him. "Good night."

Amity prepared for bed with a lighter heart, silently thanking God for the respite. By the time Aunt Enid joined her an hour later, she had folded her things into a semblance of order and was reading in bed.

She raised her brows at her aunt. "I like Clem. Why didn't you go meet him tonight?"

Enid sat on her bed and pulled her shoes off. "Believe me,

dear, it wasn't your fault. I had no intention of meeting him, even if you hadn't come."

Amity watched as her aunt fussed with blankets. "At the risk of seeming to pry, which is exactly what I'm doing, you are attracted to him, aren't you?"

"I've been attracted to men before."

"And. . . ?"

"And it wouldn't work, that's all." She shrugged. "Clem has a lovely teenage daughter who can't decide whether she wants to run from me or turn and scratch my eyes out."

"She's jealous?"

Enid pulled the sheet back on her bed and fluffed her pillow. "Who but Danielle knows? That's her name. And she's as pretty as her name. And sweet. . .as long as her father keeps his distance from me."

Amity smiled. "He doesn't seem to be taking her hints. What does he do for a living?"

"He's a horse rancher." Enid pulled a nightgown out of her bureau. "Only three of his horses, though, are taller than your waist. He breeds miniature horses, most of them growing no taller than two feet."

"Perfect," Amity declared. "You love horses."

"I love to ride horses, not hold them in my lap. Clem also portrays Pilate in The Great Passion Play up at the Christ of the Ozarks. He and Titus are both in it. Titus plays Peter. That's why the beard and hair."

"He told me. Last fall he'd mentioned something about wanting to do that. I'm glad he did."

"Did he also tell you he's helping with the New Holy Land project, since he's been to Jerusalem and knows the Holy Land?"

"Is there anything he can't do?"

"He's not much good at cooking, although he tries sometimes. And for a college professor, he doesn't know much about women. He's thirty and I doubt he's been on very many dates. You were an exception last year."

"You're making me feel really good," Amity said dryly.

"Just being honest. You know he's painfully shy around women, especially eligible single women. He's always been so serious about his college, and then his career, he didn't take the time for much social contact. Now I think maybe he's afraid the opportunity is passing him by. People have asked me what's wrong with him that he's never been married. But then, they ask me the same thing about myself."

"There's nothing wrong with either of you."

Enid hugged her niece. "Thanks. Sometimes I wonder. Try to get some sleep now. Everything will look better in the morning."

&

The next morning the tantalizing aroma of frying bacon awakened Amity from a blissfully deep sleep. She stretched her arms lazily above her head, yawned, and then just lay there, enjoying the feeling of security, snuggled beneath the blankets, with the knowledge that along with her fiercely loyal aunt, a big, healthy man was somewhere below, guarding her.

Birds sang and squirrels chattered in the huge oak tree outside an open window and she was tempted to drift back to sleep. But the delicious aromas persisted in rising up from the kitchen to tease her appetite.

She had not eaten since early yesterday, having been too frightened to stop on the road. After a shower, she pulled on blue jeans, an article of clothing Chad had always despised, and a turquoise cotton blouse. After making her bed, she slipped on a pair of comfortable moccasins and went downstairs.

The clinking of china and silverware reached her ears before she pushed open the swinging doors to find Enid and Titus at a long table, set in a large dining room connected to the kitchen.

"Good morning, sleepyhead," Enid called. "Dish up and have a seat. The food's in those hot plates along the counter."

"I remember," Amity said as she picked up a plate and walked toward a counter laden with food. "I thought you had a lot of boarders. Where is everybody?"

"It's early yet. Titus and I are the only ones not on vacation."

Amity looked around at Titus. "I'm afraid to ask, but did you find anything?"

"Nothing, but it was only a quick search, a first run-through."

With combined feelings of relief and frustration, Amity selected bacon, scrambled eggs, and sliced oranges before sitting down between Enid and Titus. She bowed her head, sent up a silent prayer, and looked back at Titus. "Now what?" she asked.

"I'll go through the papers again," he said. "But meanwhile you should stay close to the house, try to relax, and don't let your imagination run wild."

"That'll be hard for her," Enid said. "An active imagination runs in her family. She's a wonderful artist and when she was a little girl she used to paint pictures of dragons and monsters and things that she thought would go bump in the night. She was always afraid of the dark; I don't know if she still is or not." Enid turned teasing eyes toward her niece.

"I'm not afraid of the dark anymore," Amity said. "I'm just afraid of things that go bump in the night." She held her aunt's gaze and they both fell silent.

"You're an artist," Titus said. "That would be a great way to take your mind from more disturbing thoughts. You picked a perfect time to come here. Eureka Springs is an artist's paradise in the springtime."

"So I noticed last night," Amity replied. "Even in the dark I found a couple of places I'd love to paint. . .but I think I'll wait."

Titus finished his coffee and got up from the table. "Good idea, at least until Enid or I can go with you." He stacked his dishes and carried them to the sink. "But right now I have to see a man about a Jeep."

"Haven't they fixed that thing yet?" Enid complained. "They've had it for a week."

"Parts. They had to send to Missouri for parts. The thing's getting old, just like I am," Titus replied.

"Hmph. At thirty, you're not stooped too low yet."

"Do you have far to go?" Amity asked, eager to repay him for his help. "Maybe I could give you a ride."

Titus shook his head as he walked toward the door. "Thanks, but I have some other errands to do downtown, and it's only a couple of blocks." He turned back from the door. "Besides, I meant what I said about you staying close to the house until we find out what's going on." With a wave, he walked out. Amity sat staring after him.

"I'd do what he says, honey," Enid said as she stood up and stacked the few dirty dishes. "He has a lot of common sense."

"I know he's right." Amity frowned and bit her lip. "Aunt Enid, do you and Mom call each other every Monday like you used to?"

"Just like always."

"Then when you call her today, please don't mention anything to her about this. I don't want Mom and Dad to worry."

"Don't you think they'll wonder where you are?"

"Not for a while yet."

Enid regarded Amity thoughtfully. "You're sure you don't want them to know?"

"Not yet. Not until they have to."

Enid shrugged. "Okay, I won't say anything. But if things get worse, I can't promise not to do all I can to keep you out of danger, even if it means telling the whole city of Eureka Springs, the FBI, and the Green Berets."

Amity gave her aunt a quick hug. "Thanks. I couldn't wish for a better friend."

three

Enid motioned for Amity to follow her out the back door of the house. "Remember my view of the valley?" She slid open a plate glass partition and stepped out onto a new redwood deck.

"I know it's not quite in keeping with the Victorian theme," she said, "but it's a wonderful place for peace and solitude." She reached across and brushed a strand of Amity's long hair away from her face. "And I think peace and solitude are the things you need right now. Am I right?"

Amity gazed out at the panoramic view of Eureka Springs, with a profusion of green trees and flowers of every color. "Yes, as always. I can't stop being afraid."

"I know, honey. Look." Enid pointed across the valley to the tree-covered mountains. "See the statue of Christ, standing waist high in the trees?"

Amity saw the gleaming white statue, its arms spread out against the sky as if in welcome. Her gaze traveled over the statue and mountains to the valley again. Enid's house was built on a hillside, and Amity could see the private flower gardens in the backyards below them.

Enid cleared her throat. "I know you don't want to think about this, but I still don't think Farris is harmless. You have money she feels should be hers, and from what I've seen of human nature, money is usually behind a large percentage of the crimes committed in this world."

Amity sat down on one of the lawn chairs and lay her head back. "If she were planning to kill me, she wouldn't have come into this house last night and told Titus her name."

"Maybe not, but I still don't trust her, and it'll take a lot to convince me otherwise. Stay right there and I'll be right back."

Amity had her eyes closed against the dappled sunlight when Enid returned, a folded easel and canvas in one hand, watercolor paints and brushes in the other.

"Why didn't you tell me what you were doing?" Amity exclaimed, jumping up to help her aunt. "I could have brought them down myself."

Enid set the easel in position. "It's a good thing I had this deck built, because I have a feeling you'll be spending a lot of time out here." She sat down in Amity's vacated chair and watched her set up.

Amity lay out the brushes and spread newspapers beneath her work area. "I know the statue has been painted thousands of times, but maybe not from here, in this particular position."

As she worked, and finally touched the canvas with the deep azure of the Ozark sky, her body lost its tenseness. Two hours later she looked up with surprise when Enid appeared beside her, holding out a tall glass of iced tea, beads of water dripping from it onto the newspaper below.

"Break time, kiddo," Enid announced. She peered at Amity's unfinished painting and nodded. "I was telling Titus the truth when I said you were a wonderful artist. It's going to be good, I can tell. But then, I could be prejudiced."

Amity waved away the compliment as she accepted the glass and stepped over to one of the lounge chairs. "I don't know about that, I just know how much I love it." She took a long, cool swallow of the sweet tea and leaned back against the soft cushions.

The fresh scent of dew-washed grass and flowers was as heady as the most expensive perfume, and she breathed deeply. "Aunt Enid, no wonder you stay here. It's so beautiful." She inhaled again. "It truly is an artist's paradise." The fragrance of honeysuckle drifted up to capture her in its spell. "I wish it were possible to paint a fragrance."

Enid laughed. "Some artists who have been here seemed

to think it was possible. I never saw such a mess of 'modern' painting in my life. Give me something I can recognize anytime."

A trellis laden with purple clematis grew alongside the deck and a blackbird landed there, hanging onto the wire with its claws and beak. Ignoring his human observers, he preened inky black feathers, turned iridescent green by the sun.

The shiny blackness of those feathers reminded Amity forcibly of Chad. His hair had been black, so shiny it glowed with the same lights that shone in his hard blue eyes when he was drunk and taunting Amity. She shuddered and looked away.

Enid picked up Amity's empty tea glass. "Time to get back to your painting. If it can keep your mind away from your personal monsters, you'd better keep at it. I think Chad's death has affected you more than you think. That and the way he treated you when he was alive." She ambled back to the door and slid it open. "I'm going to start lunch. Titus should be here anytime, and I think he has to work this afternoon."

Amity stood up and walked back over to her easel. "He has to work this afternoon and tonight, too?"

"Not tonight. This is Monday. They don't have the play on Mondays. This is a good time for him to work on the New Holy Land." She stepped inside, then turned back. "Say, would you mind having dinner with Titus alone tonight? We don't have anyone staying here, so I could either fix something ahead, or the two of you could go out to dinner, my treat."

Amity raised a brow. "Matchmaking again? I thought I convinced you not to do that."

"I'm doing nothing of the sort," Enid protested. "Clem is taking two of his miniature horses to a show this evening and he's insisting I go with him. I'm afraid if I turn him down this time, he'll just throw me over his shoulder and dump me in back with the horses."

Amity laughed. "I believe if he decides to marry you, you

won't have any say in the matter."

"Wanna bet?" Enid declared with a toss of her head. "It's still a law that the woman has to say 'I do' before a man can marry her. Well, I don't, and it's going to stay that way."

Amity picked up her brush once more. "But you're going out with him tonight. Sounds to me like his caveman tactics are working. Besides, you've created your own little family right here in this house. What difference would there be in doing this, and marrying Clem?"

The front door squeaked open and closed and Enid darted a glance toward the front. "Uh-oh, here comes Titus now, and I haven't even started lunch."

"You didn't answer my question," Amity called after her retreating aunt.

❧

That evening, in deference to Enid, Amity agreed to walk to dinner with Titus. The clanging bells of a trolley car coming up the hill reached Amity's ears as the two of them strolled along the uneven sidewalks. Amity felt safe with Titus and the feeling exhilarated her after the ordeal of the past few weeks.

Her hand grazed something at the edge of the sidewalk and she looked down to find an old-fashioned iron rail encircling a tiny terrace garden. Delicately scented iris and brightly colored tulips grew around a little patch of freshly mown grass. There was just room enough for the set of white wrought-iron garden furniture.

Denying a strong urge to stop Titus and climb down a set of wobbly looking steps to that terrace, Amity contented herself with inhaling the sweet fragrance emanating from it. Perhaps later she could ask permission to come and paint this little garden. It seemed so secluded, so peaceful, so inviting. It was the essence of Eureka Springs.

The late evening sun warmed Amity's skin, a gentle breeze blew softly against her face, and she was suddenly passionately glad to be alive. "Mmmm, springtime has to be the most beautiful time of the year here."

Titus smiled. "It is. Until you've been here in the summer-
time. Nothing arouses the senses like a good, hot sun. Then,
of course, there's autumn, when all the trees turn into flaming
masses of color and the townsfolk have their arts and crafts
festival."

Unaccustomed laughter bubbled up within her. She felt
happier than she had in months. In fact, the last time she had
felt this kind of uncomplicated enjoyment with another
human being was when she had last spent time with Titus.
She shot a glance at him. Kindness seemed to emanate from
his face. . .that, and something else. . .self-confidence wasn't
the word exactly. . .it was something more than that. It was
confidence in God. His faith in God ran deep, as she had discovered early in their relationship.

"Winter is probably the best season of all," she said. "Isn't
that when everything quiets down and the natives have
Eureka Springs to themselves once again?"

"I can tell Enid's been talking to you," Titus said. "Speaking
of arts and crafts, I saw the picture you're doing out on the
deck. It's very good. Are you planning to finish it this week?"

"I hope to."

"You can probably sell your work in one of the shops downtown in just a few days."

Amity glanced up at him with uncertainty.

He nodded. "Not only is there plenty here to stir the imagination, but there are people who will buy your work when
you're finished. I know several shopkeepers downtown who
will take your work on consignment." He grabbed an overhanging branch and pushed it out of her way. "When they sell
your picture, you get paid. If you want to continue painting,
I'll find someone to take your work."

"You really think people will buy them?"

Titus glanced at her in surprise. "Of course they'll buy
them. You're very good. Don't tell me you've never sold any

of your work before."

"No. I've always considered it a hobby. If you'll remember, last year I was auditioning for a new part on stage."

"And did you get one?"

"No, I. . .met Chad."

"And he didn't want you to pursue a career?"

"No."

"Ordinarily, I would say that was good, but I know how much you wanted to be an actress last autumn. How about now? Do you still want to act?"

Amity hesitated. "I don't know. It's almost like I'm a different person now, Titus. I want different things."

"What kinds of things?"

She shot him an amused glance. For someone who was painfully shy around women, he was becoming less shy as the night continued. It almost felt as if they were slipping back into their comfortable friendship of last fall, before the folks decided Titus was going to become their son-in-law.

"Amity?" he pressed. "What kinds of things?" His steps slowed.

"Something more substantial than what I'd had in mind then. . .something serving God. I've learned that much these past few months. Nothing matters unless God is the pivot point of my life."

A slow, warm smile entered his eyes. "You've changed, Amity."

With a loud rumble and whining of gears, an old-fashioned, open-air trolley car came up the street behind them.

"Are you tired of walking?" Titus asked.

"No, but I would like to ride on one of those. I've wanted to ever since I saw them from the deck this morning."

"Okay, then, all aboard," he announced as he waved for the little green bus to stop.

Its brass bell clanged; Amity smiled at the conductor and climbed aboard. When she and Titus found seats, she turned to him. "Is it fun to be in the Passion Play?"

His expression became serious as he stared out into the dense foliage alongside the street. "Fun is a weak term for it."

He stretched an arm across the rail behind her and grasped a leaf as the car rumbled up the narrow street. "Exciting, enthralling, uplifting. . ." The breeze blew his dark hair away from his face. "That would more aptly describe it." He glanced at Amity thoughtfully. "Would you like to be in it for a night?"

"Me?" She sat up straighter in her seat. "In the play?"

"Yes, as a part of the crowd. But first you probably want to see the play again."

"I'd love to."

"If you want, I'll take you sometime this week." He fell silent as the trolley rounded a sharp, hairpin curve. They entered what appeared to be a tunnel of green, with the street completely overhung by trees and vines. Amity had driven this way when she had come in last night, but it looked totally different in the daylight.

"Would you be interested in acting again if it were something you considered substantial?" Titus asked.

She spread her hands helplessly. "Right now I'm in limbo. I can't make any decisions." She regarded him in silence for a moment. Had he been reading her thoughts? She truly did want to go back to the kind of work she had done before, and he could not know how much The Great Passion Play appealed to her.

"But you don't have to make any decisions. Would you like to act again?"

"If I had a role like yours, I would love to act. I'm just not sure about my future right now." She could not tell him all of it, not yet. Not about the uneasiness she felt about her body, about the nausea, the dizziness, and the questions that rose in her mind that she persisted in pushing away.

They passed a sign that read: CRESCENT HOTEL, 1886 and their vehicle turned toward the entrance. The little brass bell clanged a warning to pedestrians, who paid little heed, but darted across its path as it coasted to a stop.

Titus stood up and extended his hand to Amity to help her down. "Come with me, I want to show you a good view of the valley."

She took his hand and peered out at the building. They had visited the Crescent Hotel last autumn, but only for dinner at the restaurant. It was built of weathered gray stone, its lines gracious and inviting. It was surrounded by blooming flower gardens, and by people.

A pair of mottled gray horses, pulling a bright red surrey, stepped up alongside the trolley. As Amity and Titus stepped to the ground, a young couple climbed aboard the surrey and rode off amidst the jingle of reins and snorting of horses.

Titus escorted Amity up shallow, stone steps through the front door of the hotel, where the sight of men and women clad in casual jeans, shorts, and bathing suits, contrasted with the huge, high-ceilinged room. The room was trimmed in century-old, polished mahogany, and decorated with what Amity was sure must be authentic pieces of Victorian furniture.

Titus guided her through the crowded room to a wide, richly carpeted stairway, and she trailed her hand up a heavy, polished, wooden banister. "Just think, this place is one hundred years old," she murmured as they reached the first landing where a large, round mirror, gilded in bronze, hung on the wall. Amity glanced into it to find Titus's gaze resting on her.

His eyes held an expression of wonder, as if he had just opened a special gift. "This way," he said, leading her up more steps.

Amity caught her breath with delight when they reached the broad sundeck on the third floor. She stepped gingerly across to the heavy pipe railing and gazed out over the rolling, tree-covered mountains. Not only could she see for miles across the countryside, but the whole town was spread out before her, each brightly painted house and building placed in a setting of greenery.

Titus gestured toward the sculptured gardens and the swimming pool below them. "Watch the children playing in the water. Being with children always soothes my mind. They take up my interest so completely that the adult world of care and worry vanish for a while."

Amity leaned over the railing and smiled at the laughing, boisterous swimmers, splashing each other and screaming. Then she looked across at Titus and noted his rapt expression.

"You really do love them, don't you?" Amity asked.

"Very much," Titus answered. "They're an endless source of fascination to me, watching them grow and develop their individual talents, especially when they're been nurtured in the right way, in a Christian atmosphere."

Over the sounds of the splashing waters of the pools and fountain, Amity could hear the sweet singing of a mockingbird and a faint tinkle of nearby wind chimes, which were as characteristic of Eureka Springs as the tiny terrace garden had been.

The sky gradually lost its brightness and, as Amity watched, some of the parents called their children in from their play.

Titus turned to Amity. "Hungry?"

"Starved," she answered.

"Then let's go eat," he said, leading the way back inside.

To Amity's delight, Titus hailed the little red surrey when they stepped back outside. He helped her up and they sat down in comfortable, cushioned leather as they rolled off to the steady *clop-clop* of the horses' feet.

The sun, by this time, was merely a reflection of pink against lingering silver clouds, and heavy foliage often obscured this. The flitting shadows of swallows played across the sky, dipping and gliding as they caught their dinner. Far too soon for Amity, the driver pulled his horses to a stop, and Titus jumped down to help her out.

After he paid the driver, Titus guided Amity up a flagstone sidewalk to an unpretentious log cabin bearing a sign that announced its name, "Pig in a Poke." Smoke puffed up beside the building from three, fifty-five-gallon drums that had been turned into barbecue grills. Amity caught the tantalizing whiff of roasting meats just as Titus opened the squeaking door and held it open for her.

The small dining area was filled with people sitting at wooden tables spread with red gingham tablecloths. To the right, a long table, laden with food, was set along an unfinished log wall. Amity's mouth watered at the wonderful smells, and they soon filled their plates with more than either of them could finish.

Twenty minutes later, Titus glanced at Amity and laughed. He dipped a napkin into his water and descended on her chin. "You need a quick course in rib eating, city girl."

"Oh? Who made you the expert?" She met his teasing eyes with warm laughter in her own, and silently mused at the change in circumstances in the last twenty-four hours. Last night she had been alone, frightened, lost. And now. . .now she had her friend. . .a good friend. . .back from last year and his shyness was all but gone for tonight. She knew it could resurface tomorrow, when he would be self-conscious again. Maybe that would not happen. Maybe this wonderful sense of companionship and joy could last.

He finished wiping her mouth, put down his napkin, and stood. "I'll be right back. It's time for dessert."

"No!" she protested quickly. "I'm stuffed. I don't think I could swallow another bite." She patted her stomach for emphasis.

"We'll see," he said with a mischievous grin as he strode toward the dessert table.

She grew thoughtful as her eyes rested on his tall, muscular frame. The season had just begun and his face and arms were already tanned, as if he had been spending a lot of time in the sun. As befitted his open, friendly manner, his clothing was casual, with nicely fitting blue jeans and a navy blue cotton pullover. Try as she might, Amity could not remember him in a three-piece suit, clean shaven, and with short hair.

He strolled back to the table, a mischievous grin on his face.

Amity's eyes widened when she saw the heaping dish of strawberries and whipped cream he set in front of her. "Haven't you ever heard of moderation?"

"Now, now," he soothed. "Admit it, if I hadn't brought you your own dish, you'd have eaten mine."

Unable to resist, she bit into a ripe, sweet strawberry covered with fluffy whipped cream. "Probably."

He soon devoured his, and when she had eaten her fill and pushed her dish away, he started in on hers.

The tiny dining room gradually emptied and Amity discovered there was another room farther back. A group of laughing teenagers walked through the doorway and stood in a growing line at the cash register.

"If teaching is so great, why did you quit?" Amity asked as Titus laid his napkin down for the last time.

"It's a rewarding way of life, but not the only way," he responded.

"So what now?" she inquired.

He took a long swallow of ice water. "I spent six years teaching college students in Texas the basics of Christian elementary education. I want to see if I know what I've been talking about."

"In other words, you want to teach younger children."

He nodded. "I've done it before, on a strictly unofficial basis, and I loved it."

"You never told me where you first became interested in Christian elementary education. You're an only child, right? Just like me."

"That's right. We had an orphanage at the mission in Texas. That was where I realized a call to work with children. Too many people take education too lightly."

"Not everyone. You should meet my parents," Amity said dryly. "They refused to let me work or have a car, or practically even date until I graduated from college. How are your folks doing? Are they still in Corpus Christi?"

"Yes, they started another orphanage in Corpus Christi and they receive a lot of help with it from their church."

"So this year has been a sabbatical for you to work at the Passion Play and advise them about the New Holy Land. I'm sure they appreciate your expertise. Didn't you say you'd lived there for a year?"

"Yes. I did some special studies there, just out of my own interest. It's coming in handy now, and I flew back there this past winter to check on some of my facts. We have a project of miracles in our New Holy Land. I would love to take you there."

"And I would love to go." The idea excited her, not only because she had always been interested in the Holy Land, but because she loved the prospect of spending more quality time with Titus.

What was happening here? It suddenly seemed as if their relationship had picked up where it had left off last fall, and then taken a giant leap forward. At least, it seemed that way to Amity. As for Titus. . .she glanced at him, and found him watching her again, with that sense of awe in his expression. Maybe. . .

The waitress brought their check and Titus got up to go pay. The line at the cashier counter had grown longer and Amity sat watching the people while she waited for Titus to return.

She smiled to herself as she watched the expressions on the faces of people who had obviously eaten too much. More diners emerged from the back room and Amity took another sip of water as she studied them.

Then her hand froze on her glass. Her breath caught in her

throat and her eyes widened in alarm as she sighted a slender, black-haired woman coming through the door. It was Farris, and she looked at Amity immediately, as if she were not surprised.

Amity's blue eyes narrowed. Farris looked so much like Chad that Amity felt herself tremble.

Farris started across the room toward her.

four

"Hello, Farris," Amity said. "What brings you to town?"

Farris looked Amity over with cool appraisal as she approached and stopped in front of her. "A little red address book I just happened to find on your kitchen counter, with a Eureka Springs address circled in green."

Amity nearly groaned aloud. So that was what had happened to it! How could she have been so stupid? In her haste with packing, she had left the most important item—the most dangerous item—right there for anyone to see.

"You didn't happen to bring it with you, did you?" she asked Farris.

"It's in my suitcase." Farris studied Amity's face, as if searching for a clue about what Amity was thinking. "What happened, did it get too hot for you and your friends in Oklahoma City?" She leaned closer. "Are they hiding out with you here?"

"Who are you talking about?"

"Save the innocent act," Farris snapped. "Weren't your father's millions enough for you? Or maybe 'Daddy Dear' wouldn't turn loose of enough to please you. I bet it was a shock when you found out about the trust."

"Not at all. It made perfect sense to me. For an accountant, your brother sure didn't know how to handle money. He knew how to spend it, though."

"Oh, he had help. Lots of help."

"Not from me, Farris. Give it a rest, will you? I didn't spend—"

"I've got evidence on the rest of them, and I'll get it on you, too, before I'm finished. I'll blow this thing sky-high."

Amity stared at her in silence, barely aware of the curious stares they attracted. "Evidence about what?"

"Don't play innocent with me!" the woman spat. "You're into it up to your eyebrows, or he would've given you those papers instead of me. My baby brother knew I never approved of his lifestyle."

"What papers?"

Farris's angry gaze raked Amity up and down. "You pretend to be so pious your feet don't touch the ground. What'll the police say. . .what'll your precious church say. . .when they discover you were so greedy you helped kill your own husband?"

Amity reached out blindly toward the table for support and knocked over her water glass. She heard the thud and felt water splash against her arm but she kept her gaze riveted on Farris.

"Then it wasn't suicide," she croaked.

Farris took another step toward Amity. Farris's face flushed and her jaw muscles were working convulsively, as if she were trying not to cry. Maybe Farris had cared something about her brother, after all.

"You know Chad didn't kill himself," she hissed. "I tried to warn him about you but he wouldn't listen. I guess he's paying for it now." As she spoke, she leaned closer and closer to Amity until their faces were inches apart, but Amity refused to back away.

"What's going on here?" Titus's voice seemed to come from far away as Amity shook her head to clear her muddled brain. She looked at Farris, whose chest rose and fell with labored breathing, her eyes still fixed on Amity.

Titus took Farris by the arm. Farris jerked away and raised a hand as if to strike him. "Touch me again and I'll scream!" She took a step backward, looking from him to Amity.

Was that fear Amity saw in her sister-in-law's eyes?

Titus followed Farris. "Miss Edmonds, I don't know what

you want from Amity, but you'll have to go through me to get to her from now on. I suggest you find your way back to Oklahoma City."

"Not until I'm finished here." She swung away and shoved the door open. It slammed behind her as she disappeared into the darkness.

Amity realized the whole dining room had fallen silent. Diners had stopped eating and were watching Titus and Amity.

Titus took her by the arm. "Let's go before they ask for an encore." He bowed toward the crowded room and led Amity out the door.

As they stepped out into the cool night air, Amity had to concentrate to keep her knees from buckling beneath her. She gulped a lungful of fresh, reviving air. "She thinks I killed Chad," she told Titus.

Titus slowed his steps. "Maybe she's just trying to scare you."

"She meant it. She really thinks I killed her brother, I could see it in her eyes." Amity stopped in the middle of the sidewalk and faced Titus. "She says she has the papers. They must be what the intruder was looking for in my house. She says she already has evidence on the rest of them."

"The rest of whom?"

Amity shrugged helplessly and turned to walk through the darkened town, picking her way over uneven sidewalk, around bushes that had grown out toward the street.

"Apparently, Chad must have sent her something," Amity said. "But what? What kinds of papers?" She put her hand to her forehead. "Why didn't he ever tell me anything? All he ever mentioned were his 'friends,' who he said could make me sorry if I left him. And that was when he was drunk. I don't think I really believed him completely. Not when he was alive."

"You're probably tired of the question, but why didn't you leave him when he mistreated you?" Titus asked as they stepped beneath a canopy of overhanging trees.

Amity tugged a single leaf from one of the branches and fingered it absently. "Divorce is wrong, Titus. Don't you believe that?"

"Yes, I do, but so is murder. If you were in danger—"

"I know. Maybe it was just some silly, idealistic dream I had that showing him God's love in my own life could change him. Almost as soon as we were married, I realized it was a mistake. He wasn't at all what I thought he was. But I guess, like every new bride, I tried to hold onto the dream." She stepped over an uneven piece of concrete. "You know, he even had my pastor fooled, so I guess I can't blame myself too much. When we went for premarriage counseling, he displayed such a knowledge of the Bible that Pastor Hankey was taken in just like I was. But Chad's knowledge changed to cynicism after we were married. Cynicism and just plain cruelty. It was as if some dark spirit in him hated the Spirit in me and was set on destruction."

"And you discovered he was an alcoholic?"

"Yes."

They walked in silence for a few moments, then Amity sighed. "I was foolish enough to believe that if I was a strong Christian witness for him, he would have a change of heart. But it didn't work that way. He would drink, then belittle me for my beliefs. He kept on and on until I lost my temper and defended myself, then he would tell me I was a hypocrite because I lost my temper." She grimaced. "And now he's dead, maybe murdered."

"How hard do I have to try to convince you to stay around close to The Annalee for the next few days? Or at least, stay close to me."

"Sounds like good advice." And a very attractive idea.

❧

Staying near The Annalee turned out to be easy because Amity found enough to keep her occupied with her paints and easel by just gazing off the back deck. With encouragement from Enid and Titus, she buried herself in her work, taking time out to relax and help Enid with an increasingly successful business, and to sit on the deck with Titus in the mornings, reminiscing about their time together last fall. They compared childhood memories and discovered a lot of things in common, such as family devotion times after dinner and close relationships with their parents. Titus seemed content to stay around the house, a fact that Enid mentioned to Amity with equal degrees of hope and encouragement.

The following Saturday Enid opened up two more guest rooms and with the added work she depended on Amity to be there when she was not to help with guests as well as with the cooking and cleaning. Amity was so busy that another week passed before it occurred to her that she had not even seen downtown Eureka Springs or that she had three paintings finished, which Titus had promised to help her sell.

Early Saturday morning, the aroma of freshly perked coffee reached her from the kitchen and she wandered in to find Enid, sitting back in a chair and reading the paper while Titus dished himself a plate of bacon, mushroom, and egg casserole. Amity greeted them both with a smile and sat down at the table with a cup of coffee.

Enid stared pointedly at Amity's cup. "Have you had breakfast?"

Amity glanced at the sideboard, laden with food, and felt her stomach roll sickeningly. "Um. . .not yet." She avoided her aunt's worried gaze. "I'll have some later. Would anyone like to go with me downtown? It just occurred to me that I haven't been there yet."

"No, and don't change the subject," Enid retorted, sounding very much like her sister, Amity's mother. "Have you suddenly taken a dislike to my cooking? This is the fourth time you've missed breakfast in the past five days. You're looking peaked. You need to eat."

Amity took a sip of coffee and pushed frightening suspicions from her mind. "Your cooking is wonderful, as always," she assured her aunt, still avoiding her eyes. "I guess I've just fallen back into my old habit of skipping breakfast."

"As well as lunch and dinner, half the time? I know you're worried, but you've got to keep up your strength. Believe me, you'll feel better with a balanced meal in your stomach."

"Don't worry. I'll grab something downtown later."

Enid shook her head. "Sure, you will. You'll eat junk. You're not going alone, are you? I have boarders for breakfast, so I can't go with you."

"I'll go," Titus said. "I have to pick up my Jeep, anyway."

"Good, then I'll give you a ride," Amity said, relieved. "I need to take the car out before it thinks I've abandoned it. Did you ever talk to that friend of yours about my paintings?"

"Sure did, last week. He's eager to see them. We can take them down anytime."

"I have three. Will that do for starters?"

"It'll do fine. Are you still interested in going to the Passion Play?"

"Yes. Tonight?"

Titus nodded. "I was going to take you sooner, but I wanted to wait until I had time to show you around the grounds before the play. You didn't see everything last fall. We've been busy these past two weeks, going over the plans and settings to make the New Holy Land as close to the real thing as possible." He carried his stacked dishes to the sink, ran water over them, and walked toward the door. "I'll meet you on the front porch in fifteen minutes, if that's time enough."

"Plenty," Amity said with a grin and then watched him walk out through the swinging doors.

"You've spent a lot of time with Titus this past week," Enid observed as she loaded the dishwasher. "He likes your company."

"Good. I like him."

Enid raised a questioning brow.

"Don't make Mom and Dad's mistake," Amity warned. "I like him. I really like him. I look forward to spending time with him. He makes me laugh. We have fun together. And I trust him and his judgment. He's a buddy."

"But not the kind of man to sweep you off your feet with poetry and sly wit," Enid said. "Like Chad."

"I don't know how a man could sweep a woman off her feet without first putting his arms around her. Titus has barely touched me. You know, it's amazing, Aunt Enid, but I find that very attractive. I guess I've really changed."

"I know what you mean. Clem attracted me first because he was a kind, warm human being. Now that he's decided he likes me as a person, he's decided to get to know the woman. I think Titus is discovering he likes the person, Amity Hudson. His interest cuts through physical attraction. He looks at the heart."

Amity smiled as she stood up and cleared some dishes from the table. "Titus King is the kind of man any woman would love to have a relationship with. I'm content to be his friend."

"For now," Enid suggested.

"I don't know what's in my future right now, Aunt Enid, if I even have a future. Let's not complicate things."

A few moments later, Amity joined Titus on the front porch and they walked down the sidewalk, shaded for the most part by tall old pines, maples, and oaks. Wind chimes tinkled from a sculptured gable at the corner of the house. She paused to inhale the fragrant air, full of springtime, before getting into her car and unlocking the door for Titus.

"I've traipsed up and down these hills many times in the past few months," Titus said as he pressed the button that brought his window down. "But it keeps changing. Every time I travel over this road, I'm overwhelmed by its beauty. Eureka Springs is a fairyland."

Enchanted, Amity drove slowly down the narrow, curving street, which was alive with flowers and greenery. They passed tiny roadside gardens planted beneath outcropping rocks, seeping with water. Occasionally, they glimpsed a gardener at work with his plants, carefully weeding, spraying, and even talking to them.

The buildings, many of them a century old, edged the street, some of them hewn into the rock of the hillside. Stairs wound up the sides of some, leading to the back where a few of the shopkeepers still lived, and flower boxes rimmed many of the alleyways and walkways. Eureka Springs in the springtime was awash with flowers.

Shop windows advertised pottery, tintype pictures, jewelry, and just about every other ware imaginable. They vied with each other for Amity's attention until she could resist no longer.

"I hope you don't mind if I stop here for a few minutes," she told Titus when she spotted a parking space and pulled up next to the curb. "I can't ignore the temptation any longer."

"This is fine, since my friend's shop is on the next corner," he said. He got out to pay the meter. "Why don't you leave your paintings in the car for now and we can get them when we're ready to take them in."

Amity agreed, and when she joined Titus on the sidewalk, she discovered she had parked directly in front of the most diverting lure of all—a candy shop.

She gazed at an old-fashioned brass taffy puller as it pulled a coil of purple taffy in the front bay window. A fresh-faced young woman worked at a counter inside, dipping fresh, red strawberries into dark chocolate. Amity's appetite returned.

Titus chuckled at the expression on her face. "Come on, little girl, I can see I won't be able to get you past here without a taste." He opened the door of the shop and led the way inside.

Amity breathed deeply, smelling the seductive aroma of warm chocolate as it rushed in a cloud to greet them. She gazed around with a watering mouth at the fairyland of sparkling, glistening candies. Before she could stop him, Titus bought her the largest chocolate-covered strawberry in the store.

"Will that satisfy you, or will you want an ice cream cone afterward?" Titus asked, amusement lurking in his eyes as they stepped back out into the spring sunshine.

She bit into the juicy, dripping confection and wiped her mouth with a napkin that Titus had provided for her. "I'll let you know in a minute."

They strolled together up the street, amid the smoky fragrance of incense and frying foods, and the sounds of the chattering, jostling tourists who crowded the sidewalks. By mutual consent, they retrieved her paintings from the car and took them down the block to a shop called Ozark Art. A short, slender man with blond hair and blue eyes greeted Titus, then eagerly looked at Amity's paintings.

"Amity, meet David, a Roman soldier in the Passion Play," Titus said.

David shook her hand and smiled, then immediately turned his attention back to the paintings. He held the first one up to the sunlight that shone in through the front window.

"You're right, Titus. She is good." He turned to her and smiled admiringly. "Paintings of the statue are selling well this year." He held one up that Amity had done of a terrace garden. "These should sell quickly. What price are you asking?"

Amity had no idea how much to ask, so David helped her settle on a good price, then turned to Titus. "I hear you have a new understudy."

Titus nodded. "He transferred from group six last week. Can't see him putting his heart into the part, but I don't do the casting. Nelson seems like a nice guy, though. Maybe I'm just prejudiced because he has a clean shave and short hair."

"Probably. You just want everyone else to suffer for the cause of Christ. I bet that beard itches sometimes. Glad I'm a Roman soldier. Nelson from group six, huh? I thought he left the play."

"Apparently he agreed to come back when he received the understudy part."

David mentioned the work Titus was doing in the New Holy Land, and since Amity already knew firsthand from Titus how that was going, she wandered through the air-conditioned shop, admiring the paintings of other local artists and doing a quick inventory of their art supplies. Since Titus and David seemed to be engrossed in a detailed deliberation about a site for one of the hiking trails, Amity stepped outside—directly into the path of Farris Edmonds.

Farris, dressed in a tight, black miniskirt and tank top, stood with her hands on her hips, as if she had been waiting for Amity to emerge.

"Where's the National Guard today?" she taunted, glancing around them with nervous, jerky movements. "You mean they actually let you out of the house without your watchdog?"

Amity did not bother to suppress her irritation. "Would it do any good? Every time I step outside, I find you've been stalking me. Farris, this is getting old."

Farris combed nervous fingers through her hair. "It's going to get older and it wouldn't be necessary if you'd answer my calls."

"Calls?" Amity demanded. "What calls?" Farris had changed. Gone was the harsh, bitter anger that had been so evident at their last meeting. But she was still troubled. Dark circles looked like bruises beneath her striking blue eyes.

"I've called you several times from Oklahoma City." She grimaced. "Your watchdogs must think they're protecting you from some crazy woman."

"The idea did occur to them," Amity said dryly. "If you have accusations to make, make them now, and make them clear," Amity said. "I know you're unhappy about the settlement of Chad's estate but that's no reason to accuse me of murder and to stalk me all over the country."

Farris narrowed her eyes as she held Amity's gaze. "I've done some research on you and your family."

"Good. Now you know my family history is squeaky clean to the point of boredom. Would you mind telling me about these papers Chad sent you?"

Farris looked at her quickly, her arched, black brows drawing together in a frown. Then she shook her head. "I'm not ready to go that far yet."

In frustration, Amity glared at Farris. "If someone killed Chad, I want to know about it. I want the police to have the proof and I want the killer caught. I can't believe his own sister would withhold information from the police and let the trail grow cold. Someone ransacked my house, Farris. That was why I ran, not because I was guilty of anything, but because Chad's 'friends,' whoever they are, think I have something I don't have. Where are these papers you talk about?"

"I left copies of them with my attorney. The originals are in a safety deposit box."

"Did you come all the way to Eureka Springs, twice, just to tell me this?"

"I had business in Fayetteville. Uncle Jim had his pilot fly me there, and one of his associates drove me here."

"Uncle Jim?" Amity had never liked Chad's mother's brother and the sentiment had been mutual. "I thought you two never got along. If you disapproved of Chad, surely you also disapproved of your uncle. They're so much alike."

"I'm working for him now. He's running for the state senate. It's a leg up for my career."

"Yeah, right. Good ol' Uncle Jim, but don't trust him any further than you can see him. Farris, seriously, if you have proof that Chad was actually murdered, please go to the police with it. I don't know why you've held it this long."

"I have good reasons."

"What can be a good reason to let murderers get away?"

Farris's eyes narrowed. She leaned forward. "Before I go to

the police, let me see all of Chad's other papers, those he kept in the attic safe. They're numbered consecutively and I want the original master sheet. If you've taken anything out, I'll know. Chad told me about them in the stuff he sent me."

"The old CPA records? That's all you want?"

"I know you brought them with you because they weren't there when I checked your house."

"When you checked my house, you must have seen the mess someone had already made. You can't possibly think I did that."

For the first time, Farris hesitated, but she did not reply. Instead, she said, "Are you willing to let me see the papers?"

"You can have them with my blessing. I can't make any sense out of them."

"Not unless you know what to look for."

"You weren't the one who ransacked my house two weeks ago, were you?" Amity asked.

"Of course not!" Farris replied.

Amity shrugged. "You can see the papers anytime you want. There's nothing in them about Chad's 'friends,' as far as I can tell. When do you want them?"

"Now." Farris's expression showed sudden weariness. "I'm going back to Fayetteville for two weeks."

"Is someone picking you up?"

"They will when I call them."

"Don't call them. Take the BMW."

Farris raised a finely shaped brow. "You can't be serious."

"Why can't I? I have no use for the car right now, as close as I am to town. I'm not planning to leave. You can come back with me now and I'll give you the records. Will that convince you I wasn't involved in this?"

Farris looked down at her folded hands. "I'm not sure what to believe right now."

Amity did not push it. "I'll be here when you get back, unless Chad's friends followed one of us and decides to come visiting. I've been staying close to Aunt Enid's."

Farris glanced at her again, her blue eyes still uncertain. "Well, you can tell your aunt I'm not a physical threat to her precious niece. She seemed to think I was out to kill you or something."

"That's because I received some frightening phone calls in Oklahoma City. Aunt Enid thought it might be you." Amity shook her head. "I wish it had been. At least I'd know who's after me."

Farris paused, then took a deep breath and exhaled. She stared hard at Amity again. "I'm not 'after' anyone except Chad's killer. I'm still not sure I trust you."

"Chad never trusted anyone, either. Seems to run in the family. I wonder why."

Farris shrugged with impatience. "If these records prove anything, I'll probably turn Chad's confession into the police."

Amity stood with her. "It only takes one phone call."

"It's waited two months. It can wait until I see those records."

"Can't you tell me anything about it?" Amity pleaded. "Farris, my life's on the line here!"

"I want to read those records you have first."

Amity raised her hands helplessly. "Okay, I can't tell you what to do with them."

Farris watched her suspiciously. "What's in this for you?"

"I hope justice. I'm not interested in any money. I just want this whole thing far behind me. Money doesn't buy happiness."

"How would you know? You've always had money."

"But I wasn't happy until I learned to trust in God, not money."

Farris held up her hand. "Forget the sermon. You must have preached to Chad every day you two were married. He's still dead. Funny, he put a note in with the other stuff he sent me." Her gaze rested on Amity with a mixture of doubt and sadness.

"He said you had made him ashamed, that you lived your life like he'd always thought a Christian should, and you'd given him hope that someday he could be a better person, too." Farris shook her head. "That was all he said. I'm not sure what he meant, or why he said it."

Surprised that Farris had softened enough to share this information, Amity felt one of the heavy weights slide from her heart. "So, he did listen."

"Yeah, and all his good intentions died with him. I'll take that car, if you're really offering it."

five

The delectable aroma of freshly baked, homemade rolls greeted Amity when she stepped back inside the bed-and-breakfast. She had just turned over the car and the two suitcases to Farris, against Titus's advice. She entered the kitchen just as Enid took another batch of rolls from the oven.

Amity sneaked up behind her and snitched one hot, yeasty roll. The heat seared her fingers. "Ouch!" She tossed the roll from hand to hand to let it cool.

Enid aimed a playful swat of a towel at Amity's posterior. "That'll teach you."

Amity tore off a chunk of the crusty bread and put it in her mouth. "Mmmm, it was worth it," she said, closing her eyes and savoring it as she tore off another bite. "You bake the best bread I've ever eaten."

"Well?" Enid prompted as she rolled out another batch of dough onto the counter. "What happened in town? Did you sell your paintings?"

"I did better than that," Amity said. "I had a good talk with Farris and—"

"What?" Enid stared at her, aghast. "Titus allowed her near you?"

"Titus was inside talking to David and I had slipped out. When he found out what I'd been doing he wasn't too happy with me."

"I'll bet!"

"But he calmed down after I told him what I found out."

"Which was?"

Amity finished her roll and wiped her hands on a towel. "First, why didn't you tell me Farris was calling here? I wish

I had known."

Enid stopped forming rolls and turned around. "I'm sorry. I know I probably should have told you." She dusted her hands off and stepped over to stand beside Amity. "But you were so worried, and you haven't been eating." With a finger, she traced the dark circles under Amity's eyes. "I didn't feel you needed the extra strain. I just thought Farris was going to harass you, and I didn't want that. Forgive me?"

"Oh, Aunt Enid, really," Amity said. "There's really nothing to forgive. I know you're worried about me. I loaned Farris the BMW."

"What! Amity, what—"

The kitchen door swung open and Titus walked in. "I can see she told you." He tossed a package on the table. "I brought you some fudge, but it doesn't look like you're hungry."

Enid shook her head. "No, I've just lost my appetite. Amity, why would you do something like that?"

"I don't need the car but she does. She's trying to find Chad's killer. Yes, she believes he was murdered and she says she has proof. I'll help her if I can." Amity fingered the package Titus had laid on the table. "What kind of fudge?"

"Amity, how can you think of fudge at a time like this?" Enid demanded.

With an indulgent smile, Titus unwrapped the chocolate peanut butter fudge and put the squares in a bowl. "Enid, you've been wanting her to eat and now she is. Make up your mind."

Amity took a piece and put the whole thing in her mouth. It tasted delicious, rich, and buttery. "Thank you, Titus," she said with a full mouth. "It tastes even better than it smells."

Enid put her hands on her hips. "Amity Hudson, are you forgetting that woman came here to threaten you?"

"She never threatened to hurt me physically. The only thing that scared me about her was that I thought if she could find me, someone else could. She suspected that I was instrumental in Chad's death."

"She wanted to believe that," Enid retorted. "You said so yourself."

"But she has doubts now."

"There's one good thing that comes from this," Titus said, offering Amity another piece of fudge as she finished her first. "You're apparently well-hidden here. Farris must have been the only one who followed you, since you haven't received any more threatening calls. Now you can get involved in the Passion Play, get out and meet people, go to church with Enid and me."

"But Enid needs me to help here, since business has picked up so well."

"Don't worry about that," Enid said. "I can always hire part-time help. If you can get a part at the Passion Play, you take it."

"In fact," Titus said, "for the first time in years, we have a shortage of good actresses. Our Mary Magdalene is quitting in about three weeks and her understudy broke her leg."

Amity watched him with growing hope. How wonderful it would be to act again. Especially in the Passion Play!

"They may be interested in you for the part," Titus said.

Amity took a deep breath. "I'd love it."

"Then I suggest you see the play again to refresh your memory," he said.

"In that case, I'll fix dinner a little early," Enid said, giving Amity a quick hug before turning back to finish her rolls.

❧

"Tell me more about the Christ of the Ozarks," Amity suggested to Titus as they rode in his newly repaired Jeep through the historic downtown area of Eureka Springs.

Titus slowed down to allow a group of elderly pedestrians to cross the road in front of them. "What do you want to know? There are several points of interest at the site."

"Then start with the site itself." Amity craned her neck

to look into the window of a doll collection shop. "Why is it set here, in a less populated area? Why not New York, or California, where more people can see it?"

Titus turned onto a narrow paved lane and started their slow climb toward the top of a heavily wooded mountain. The lane twisted up the hill, its curves shaded by huge oak and walnut trees.

"It is beautiful here," Amity said, "with Eureka Springs nestled in amongst the trees."

"When we get to the top, you'll see why the statue is here," Titus said. "In this central location, here in these peaceful surroundings, there are more people within a thousand-mile radius than there would be in the East or West. The truth of Christ can reach more hearts from here." His voice held the tone of conviction.

The trees became more sparse as the Jeep neared a fork in the road. Without stopping, Titus turned left. To their right, Amity saw a great wall, totally constructed of huge, white blocks.

"I know I showed you a lot of this last year, but indulge me. This is the Golden Gate," Titus informed her. "It's the entrance to the New Holy Land, which you haven't seen yet. I wasn't working on it last year when you and I first met. The directors discovered I had lived in Jerusalem and they invited me to take part in the planning. They had a lot done already, but they've used my input to make some changes and to add some other areas of interest."

"I can't wait to see it," Amity said.

"And I can't wait to show it to you, but I'll have to take you there later; it covers more area than we'll have time to see today." He pulled the Jeep to a stop before one of the two arched openings in the wall. "Not one of the blocks in that wall weighs less than a ton. Our workers formed them right here on the grounds."

"That sounds like a long, slow process."

"It was. The amazing thing was that they were built into this wall without the use of mud or mortar. You can actually stand beneath the archway and see daylight between some of the blocks."

Amity laughed. "No, thanks. It doesn't sound safe to me."

"Believe me, it's safe," Titus assured her. "A ton of concrete doesn't move easily. It would take a powerful force to knock those stones loose."

At his urging, Amity did walk beneath the white, arched gateway. Once on the other side, she saw a crowd of people seated in bleachers, surrounding a central speaker dressed in the flowing robes of Jesus' day. The speaker was seated at a potter's wheel, working with a lump of unformed clay as he spoke to the crowd.

"That's the potter," Titus said, keeping his tone low so as not to disturb the listening crowd.

"I remember from last fall. He's different from the potters in town. He's teaching about the parallel between the creation of the clay pot by the craftsman and the constant growth of a Christian in God's loving hands."

"As you have grown, Amity," Titus said.

"I noticed some of the pottery shops in town today. Weird stuff, with dragons crawling out of eggs, things like that."

"In a place like this, where you find a lot of Christians, you will also find a lot of influences that are anti-Christian. It can be a shock at times."

"I'll say. But I have to remind myself that, of course, Satan wants to attack where God is working. What bothers me is that Satan likes to mimic God's creation, distorting and corrupting it, and people so often believe Satan's lies."

"But God is more powerful than Satan, Amity. Never forget that. If we remember to rely on God's power, we rob Satan of his."

A few moments later they passed back through the arched gateway and walked past ticket offices and a gift shop. They entered a narrow entryway shaded by tall pines.

The first strains of sweet music reached Amity's ears long before she and Titus neared the statue of the Christ of the Ozarks. The music emanated from some unseen speakers, strategically placed. Amity peeped up through an opening in the trees, and stared as the great white form of the statue emerged. People of all ages and nationalities milled about at the foot of it, gazing up in wonder. In spite of the crowd, Amity heard little chatter. The melodies of some of her favorite hymns floated down over them, the sound of it covering her in a blanket of peace. The fragrance of honeysuckle reached her in the gentle breeze.

"It looks as beautiful in the spring as it did in the fall," she whispered as they approached the front of the statue.

"It's seven stories tall." Titus guided her into one of the open-air gazebos, which were placed around the grassy areas for quiet meditation and rest. "Tall enough for people to see it from all over the valley."

"What a perfect setting."

"Now you see what I mean?" Titus smiled at her. "The city itself is peaceful, spread out below." He waved his arm in a sweeping gesture toward the parts of Eureka Springs that they could see. "But this is farther removed from the noises of the town."

Amity sank down onto one of the wooden benches that ringed the gazebo. She inhaled the sweet fragrance of the pansies hanging in pots from the wooden rafters and occasionally caught a whiff of the wild roses that grew along the mountainside.

"I love it," she said. "Those arms stretch out, reaching into infinity, reminding us that Jesus Christ died for all people. His salvation is not just for one specific denomination, but for everyone who trusts in him as Savior and Lord." She looked up to find Titus watching her. "Thank you," she said simply.

"You're welcome." He reached down to draw her up beside

him. "You okay?"

"Better all the time."

"You've been under a lot of stress. It won't go away overnight but this may help take your mind off things for a while."

Amity paused for another look across the valley. "I know people who would blame me for being frightened. They would say I don't have enough faith in God. Maybe they would be right."

"And maybe they would be speaking from ignorance, unless they've come through something like this themselves, without fear."

"Do you think that if I had perfect faith in God, I wouldn't be afraid?" Amity asked.

"Yes. But do you know many people who have perfect faith in God? Most of us are still striving toward that goal."

They walked back in silence, avoiding the paved lane in favor of the less-congested path along the edge of the forest. Cars now crowded bumper to bumper and the people in charge of parking them worked quickly.

They arrived back at the Jeep and Titus reached inside. "I brought you a quilt, just in case it gets cold." He handed it and a ticket to Amity. "Wait here for me when you come out. I won't be long. I may even beat you here." He smiled. "Are you looking forward to seeing the play?"

"I've heard so much about it, how could I not be?" She returned his smile. "I'll be particularly interested in Peter. Just think, I know him personally."

"That really is something," he said as he walked with her toward the entrance to the theater. "You don't even know Titus King personally. . .yet." He grinned at her, then saluted and left.

Amity descended with the rest of the crowd into the huge outdoor amphitheater. True to his word, Titus had given her a front-row seat and as she sat down, she gazed down over the play setting. It was so realistic, with the temple, the palaces, the upper rooms, and even Golgotha above the rest, on the hillside.

Dusk came and Amity looked above the city of Jerusalem to see the lighted statue of Christ, the arms still spread in loving welcome. Soft, stirring music, after creating the mood, died away. Darkness grew. Amity detected shadows flitting across the expanse of street in Jerusalem. New sounds reached her ears as she heard the *clop-clop* of horses' feet, the calling of men's voices, the bleating of lambs. The play began.

The scenes spotlighted before her touched a chord of familiarity in her mind, just as it had the last time. The person who wrote the play was in tune with her own heart. The week of passion had always mystified her with its depth of meaning. The resurrection had always drawn tears from her eyes with God's promise of hope after Christ's agonizing death.

Amity had always thought she would have liked to have been Mary Magdalene, a woman blessed by her close fellowship with Jesus Christ. Oh, to have sat there at His feet as He taught the people! The pain she had felt during His crucifixion must have vanished with tears of joy when Jesus appeared to her, alone, at the empty tomb. How she must have fallen at His feet in absolute worship!

Amity knew her eyes were moist when the play ended after the ascension, but she suspected that most of the people there were in the same predicament. Who wouldn't be moved to tears by such a beautiful reminder of God's love?

Others filed out around her while she remained in her chair, in no hurry to leave. For just a moment, after the people had cleared out, she wanted to soak up just a little more of the peace to take back with her. She needed it.

Almost all of the late stragglers cleared out. The theater had emptied with amazing speed and Amity realized with reluctance that she must leave, too. Nevertheless, maybe she could return. Maybe she could take Titus up on his offer—that is, if the directors considered her good enough.

She would, of course, love to play the part of Mary Magdalene, but any part at all would thrill her. It had been so long since those happy, carefree days before meeting Chad, when the decisions about which plays to try out for were the most major decisions she had to make. She longed to be backstage again, laughing and joking with the others in the dressing room, as happy to be just a part of the crowd as to have a starring role.

Soft benediction music played as she strolled up the aisle. The lights were low and she had not gone far when she spotted someone else remaining in his chair, perhaps listening to the peaceful music as she had.

The man glanced up at her as she walked by, then he stood, too, and stepped out behind her.

The skin on the back of Amity's neck prickled. She quickened her step, glancing out of the corner of her eye at him. She met his gaze then turned back around abruptly. He was getting closer.

The inclining sidewalk, which was so easy to walk down, was harder to climb, and she became breathless. She could still hear the footsteps of the man behind her. Was he following her?

Perspiration popped out on her brow, and she wiped it away with a swipe of her hand. She was nearing the top. Her glance darted from gate to gate and finally stopped, with relief, on a woman coming her way from the concession stand.

Then the woman waved and spoke, her chubby face creasing in a smile as she neared Amity. . .and the man behind her. "How did you like the play, honey? Did you get tired of waiting?"

Amity's body flooded with weak relief. She listened shamelessly as a couple fell into step behind her, a husband and wife, obviously, discussing the play.

Had the situation not been so tense for a moment, Amity would have laughed at herself. As it was, her heart continued to pound as her throat tightened and tears welled up in her eyes. Would it always be like this?

The rows of idling automobiles merged into a cacophony of sound, and she resisted the urge to cover her ears with her hands as she picked her way through the traffic to the Jeep. To her relief, Titus was there ahead of her, and another man leaned against the Jeep, talking. The man fell silent as Amity drew near.

Titus flashed her a smile. "Come and meet my new understudy," he said, taking the quilt from her arms and stuffing it into the back of the Jeep. "Amity Hudson, this is Nelson Bertrum, the man I mentioned earlier."

Nelson held out a hand and smiled at Amity. "I hear you're going to join our cast soon." His gaze roved over her swiftly.

"Yes. . .well, I'm going to try," she said, noting the man's easy smile. He must have to wear a wig and fake beard, since his own short, light brown hair and clean-shaven face would not work in the play. But, whether or not it was out of prejudice for Titus, she decided instantly that Nelson could never replace Titus as Peter.

Nelson went on to his own car as Titus and Amity got into the Jeep.

"Was it as good as you remembered?" Titus asked, putting the Jeep into gear. It leaped forward, rattling along the rocky driveway until they came to a halt behind a line of cars waiting to leave.

"Even better," she said. "It was as if the playwright read my thoughts and put them down on paper."

"That was because he stayed with strictly biblical accounts, and when he needed extra dialogue, he was very careful that what he used would have worked in Jesus' time."

"Not only did the playwright do a good job, but the acting was superb," Amity said. "I'll never be able to think of you as Titus King again. You're Peter to me."

"Please!" he protested with mock alarm. "Don't burden me

with that!" He grinned at her. "Which Peter am I to you, the one who denied Christ or Peter after the visit of the Spirit."

"Sorry, but it'll have to be the one who denied Jesus. You played the part so well."

The Jeep chugged forward in line with the other cars creeping toward the exit, and the sound of the motors was loud in the open-topped Jeep.

"Do you ever wonder what you would have done in Peter's place?" Amity asked, raising her voice to be heard over the noise.

Titus thought for a moment. "I think everyone who reads that account in the Bible wonders what he would do. I'm sure we all feel the same strong urge to prove that our love for Jesus is stronger than the apostle's, but in Peter's case, once Christ made the prediction, it was history. No one on earth could have changed it."

"I never thought of it that way."

Titus drove the Jeep forward once again as some of the traffic turned onto the road they had entered on. He drove straight instead of turning.

"My theory is that Peter needed the experience to teach him humility. It was a hard lesson to learn, and it might have destroyed a lesser man, but God knew how much Peter could take."

Amity frowned. "If you're saying God made Peter deny Christ, I disagree. Peter made his own choice." How good it felt to talk with a man about the things of God! How she had longed for just this kind of discussion when she was married to Chad.

"But you must agree that Jesus, as God in human form, was omniscient," Titus said. "He knew what Peter's reaction would be to the questioning court servants. Thus, with the foreknowledge of God, Peter could not have changed the flow of events. God knew Peter's weakness and He allowed those people a chance to accuse Peter, knowing what his reaction would be."

"The way He still allows us to be tested today," she said, "so we'll be able to grow." She thought about the testing she had had, herself. Was she growing now?

By now they had reached another highway and Titus turned right, heading toward town. This area was newer and less congested, mostly with motels built within the past few years to accommodate the growing tourist trade. A couple of the buildings were country music theaters.

Titus slow for an intersection, then turned right, into the older section of town. "It's been a popular place for more than a hundred years, due to the springs and the surrounding beauty. Many people in the past believed in the curative qualities of the water. Now the curative is found at the Christ of the Ozarks."

"There are curative springs there?"

"The cure I'm talking about is the Spring of Living Water that many people find in Jesus Christ while visiting here." Titus drove down the darkened Spring Street toward The Annalee. "Speaking of which, have you decided for sure if you want to try out for the part of Mary Magdalene?"

"Is the actress now definitely quitting?"

"Yes, in three weeks. As I said, her understudy has a broken leg and her second understudy, Danielle Elliot, is also understudy to Salome, who is also quitting."

"Danielle? Clem's daughter?"

"Yes. Do you want to try out for the videotape test?"

"For the Mary Magdalene part?" Amity exclaimed. "I'd love to! During the play I was thinking about how much I would have loved to have been her in Jesus' time. It would be such a thrill to go back in time and see life through her eyes."

Titus pulled the Jeep up to the curb and parked in front of Enid's house. "I know how you feel."

"Don't you find Peter a fascinating character to play?"

"Very much so."

"You are unique, Titus King," she said, surprising herself.

"Oh?" He climbed from the Jeep and came around to help her out.

"You're a Christian man who isn't afraid to talk about your love for God." Her voice was soft. "A lot of men I've known, even the guys my age at church back home, were shy about talking about the things of God. It's like they were ashamed of Him. You speak of Him with love and without a hint of shame."

"Is there any other way to speak about the One Who died for us?" Titus asked. "Are we supposed to repay His love with shame?"

They walked up the steps to the elegant front door of The Annalee. Titus opened it and ushered her in, then switched on a tiny hall light.

"I'm not unique," he said. "Maybe you've just known the wrong men in the past." He turned to face her and then stood looking at her for a long moment. "Don't you think it's time you became acquainted with the right ones?"

six

Business at The Annalee continued to increase and by Tuesday, Enid was booked every night for three weeks. Amity found little time to paint, and although she tried out for the part of Mary Magdalene, she secretly wondered if she would have time to do the part justice.

Wednesday morning a slender woman in her late fifties who had spent the night, surprised Enid, Amity, and Titus by joining them for breakfast.

"Mrs. Shrum!" Enid exclaimed, jumping up to set out another plate. "We didn't expect you for another hour at least. Most guests like to sleep in."

The woman took the seat Titus pulled out for her and accepted the cup of coffee Amity handed her. "I never sleep past six. Too much to see and do." She patted her light, sandy brown hair into place. "I like to keep active. Keeps me young."

"That's what I always say." Enid put a stack of plates on the serving table and gave Mrs. Shrum some silverware. "Help yourself, Mrs. Shrum."

"Please, call me Opal."

"Okay, Opal. There are breakfast pork chops, cheese omelets, sourdough biscuits, and fruit salad. There's enough for an army."

Opal selected an omelet, a biscuit with molasses, and sat back down. "Miss Benjamin, I'd like to make you a proposition."

"What's that?"

Opal took a sip of her coffee. "You know I'm booked to stay here for a month, but I just found out I don't have as much money as I thought I'd brought with me. I'd considered looking for a part-time job downtown, but I was wondering if you might be interested in a live-in cleaning lady for a reduction of my rent."

Enid looked hopeful. She glanced at Amity with raised brows. "You mean like doing laundry, vacuuming, dusting, stuff like that?"

"Yes, and I can also cook and look after the place if you ever want to leave."

Enid looked at Amity again, who felt as hopeful as her aunt looked. "Okay, let's see if we can work something out."

Opal looked just a little surprised, as if she hadn't really expected Enid to accept her proposal. Then she smiled and ate her breakfast with obvious appetite, even getting up to try one of the pork chops.

"Opal has been another answered prayer," Enid declared to Amity later as they peeled potatoes for the evening meal. "I think she's going to work out fine, and just in time for you to start in the play."

Amity put down her knife and rubbed her lower back. "You sound positive I'll get the part."

"Of course. The cast is good, I know, but it's been a while since they've seen an actress as good as you are. Very few of them have actually studied drama at a university."

Amity chuckled. "You sound like Mom and Dad. Don't let your prejudice show, Aunt Enid. I saw the play, remember, and they're all good."

Enid grinned. "What did you think of Titus?"

"One of the best. He's very convincing. His poor understudy doesn't have a chance."

Opal came bustling through the back door, a basketful of clean sheets in her arms. She tossed her head to get short tendrils of hair out of her eyes.

"One load to go, Miss Benjamin," she said as she strode through the kitchen. She stopped and her light blue eyes paused briefly on Amity before settling on Enid. "I was wondering if I might get off in time to go to the Passion Play tonight. I haven't seen it yet and everyone says it's good."

"Of course, Opal. I think you'll love it. And please, call me Enid." She tossed a handful of peels in a pile to save and fry later. "Mind you, the play will be much better when Amity begins her new part."

The older woman glanced at Amity inquiringly.

"Enid," Amity protested laughingly. "You'll have to excuse my aunt, Opal. She has an overabundance of family pride, I'm afraid. I just tried out for the part of Mary Magdalene and I don't even know that they're considering me yet."

Titus spoke from the doorway. "You do now."

The three women swung around to see Titus, leaning against the threshold, his pleased gaze on Amity.

She gasped. "You're sure?"

"Yes, I'm sure. I just finished talking to the director and he asked me to bring you in tonight. Are you ready?"

"Well, how about that!" Opal said brightly. "It looks like I'll be seeing your niece after all, Miss. . .er, Enid." She hefted the clothes basket higher up in her arms and walked out past Titus, toward the stairs. "Congratulations, Amity!" she called over her shoulder.

"Now that blows it," Enid said with a good-natured shrug. "I just told Opal she could be off this evening, so I can't go."

"Don't worry, you'll have plenty of time before Amity begins her part," Titus assured her. "She has to learn it first and that'll take a couple of weeks. Tonight she'll just be a part of the crowd in the marketplace."

Enid set the potatoes on the stove and wiped her hands. "I think I'll ask a friend of mine to watch this place for a couple of hours, anyway. I'd still like to be there for moral support. You go on, Amity, and get ready while I finish dinner."

❧

Two hours later, the old red Jeep once again traversed the winding climb toward the Passion Play amphitheater. This time Titus turned sooner, into the road with the cast entrance sign.

Amity fidgeted nervously with her purse and cast a sideways glance at him. Green eyes met green, hers apprehensive, his reassuring, and she smiled.

"You really don't think they'll eat me alive?" She knew there would be some women there who had tried for the part and lost to her, a newcomer. How would they accept her? The one she particularly worried about was Danielle, Clem Elliot's daughter, who was apparently already antagonistic toward Enid. How would she feel about Enid's niece knocking her out of a much-coveted part?

"You won't have to worry much about bruised egos here," Titus said. "Most of the actors and actresses are just citizens of Eureka Springs and surrounding towns, who feel this play is a part of their Christian ministry. They didn't start out in professional acting."

"So Enid says."

"Once they see you perform, they'll have to admit you were chosen for your talent, not for your association with Clem or me."

They entered the cast parking lot and Nelson Bertrum waved at them from the sidewalk. He walked over to greet them as they parked and got out.

"Congratulations, Amity, I hear you're the new Mary Magdalene." He extended his hand, and she took it with a wry smile.

"Word sure gets around fast here, doesn't it?"

He held onto her hand a moment too long and she withdrew it firmly, aware he was staring.

"Mary Magdalene is a very popular part, from what I hear," he said.

Titus took her arm and walked with her toward the huge backstage area. "Don't worry. As I said, once they see you perform, they'll know why you got it."

"Yeah, and besides," Nelson added as he stepped up to Amity's other side, "you'll have time to learn the whole play before you go on as Mary. I acted in the marketplace scenes for months before I could request an understudy position as Peter."

Titus pointed toward a dressing room door marked "Group Three." It was up one flight of heavy, wooden stairs. "You've been assigned to that group and Clem Elliot is your manager. He'll be waiting for you." He released her arm and gestured for Nelson to follow him. "Your group changes, too, Nelson."

With a growing sense of panic, Amity watched Titus leave. "Wait!"

He turned back around, amusement creasing his face.

"What group are you in?" she asked.

"Ordinarily yours, but I've switched for a few weeks. There's a man in Group Four who is studying elementary education and I'm tutoring him." He chuckled softly, his eyes caressing her face. "Don't worry, I'll be around all through the play." Still grinning, he walked her up the steps to the door and held it open while she stepped through.

To her relief, Clem was already in the dressing room. A few other early arrivals had already changed into their costumes and were sitting around on benches, talking idly. They glanced up at her with interest as she walked to the costume counter where Clem stood.

"Amity!" he greeted with his deep, growling voice. "Good to see you again." He smiled at her encouragingly, then glanced at one of the other women in the room. "Darla, would you please go find my daughter? Tell her I have a guest for her tonight."

"Sure thing, Clem." The woman stood, cast a friendly glance at Amity, and walked out.

One of the women in a far corner looked at Amity, whispered to another, and both looked up at her and smiled.

"Hey, Clem, is this our new Mary?" one of them asked.

"Yes, and wait until you see her perform," he said, winking at Amity. "Take that hunted look from your face, girl. We don't eat new actresses for dinner. Ah, here's Dani now."

Amity turned to see his daughter walk in. The teenage girl was every bit as pretty as Enid had said. Long, waving blond hair cascaded over her shoulders and was so pale it seemed to reflect the lights. Danielle's dark blue eyes met Amity's and surprised her with their glow of friendliness. The girl's blushing cheeks were barely deeper than her tanned face, and she walked toward Amity with a carefree, unaffected stride.

"Are you Amity Hudson?" Danielle asked.

"Yes, and you're Danielle?"

The girl laughed and nodded. "Dani, though, please. Nobody ever calls me Danielle. Come on over here and I'll find a costume for you." She went to the other end of the counter.

"Now that Dani's here," Clem said, "I have to go to a short meeting before we start. Don't worry. She'll take good care of you," he assured Amity as he walked out.

"They trusted me with the wardrobe tonight," Dani said, her soft voice muffled as it came from behind a long row of hanging robes and cloaks. "That's a mistake, but I'm not going to tell them that. This is the first time they've trusted me with anything like this and I think it's going straight to my head." She laughed as she emerged from the midst of the clothes with one striped robe. "This should fit." She held it up to Amity's slender form. "Come back here and we'll try it on."

Amity followed her back to the women's dressing room.

"You can wear these things over your regular clothes," Dani told Amity as they stepped into an inner room, "but it gets warm under there." Dani peeled the coat, cloak, and head covering from their hanger.

Amity unbuttoned her blouse. "That's surprising, since it got so cold up in the audience last week, but I'll take your word for it. The cast does a lot of running, don't they?"

"Yeah, it's a workout, especially for Mary Magdalene. She does a lot of running and she has to be careful, or she could fall on that concrete walk."

Amity caught her breath and, with a sinking sensation in her stomach, she darted a quick glance to Dani. "It's that dangerous? People really fall?"

Dani nodded. "Sometimes."

Amity slumped on the bench. Ordinarily, that would not bother her, but what if. . .what if those niggling suspicions she had were correct?

"It's been a while since anyone else fell," Dani continued, "but I did a couple of times. Of course, Dad says I'm clumsy as an ox."

As she dressed, Amity watched Dani for signs of resentment over losing the part of Mary, but the clear blue gaze held nothing other than easy, youthful spirits and friendliness.

"Titus tells me you're Salome's understudy," Amity remarked, pulling the heavy material of the cloak down over her head. She settled it on her shoulders and smoothed it down to her feet.

"Yes, for now." Dani shrugged. "Tomorrow night, who knows? We switch parts so that several people are used to each character. That way we're never short if someone gets sick. And since there's about two hundred people in the cast, no one misses a few out in the crowd."

"Two hundred! I didn't realize there were that many."

"It takes a lot." Dani helped Amity adjust the head covering. "I think you'll go with Darla tonight and just mill around in the street scenes to get the feel of it. If you want, when you're not in a scene, you can sit beneath the ledge."

"Can I see the play from there?"

"Most of it. Just ask Darla to show you where to go so you'll be out of sight of the audience." Dani walked over to the door and stuck her head out. "Hey, Darla! Stay there a minute. Amity's going with you tonight." She turned and explained to Amity, "I get to be the blind girl Jesus heals."

Amity draped her own clothes across a hanger and left

them in the room, then followed Dani out again into the main chamber. More people had arrived and three of them stood tapping their feet at the costume counter.

"Uh-oh," Dani murmured in Amity's ear. "They left me to work with the wardrobe and I'm goofing off." She giggled. "Oh, well. Darla, this is Amity. I'd better get up there before they try to get their own costumes and mess the whole thing up." With a toss of her long, blond hair, she dashed behind the counter.

Amity stood looking helplessly at Darla, an older, slender woman with short red hair and the most generous sprinkling of freckles she had ever seen on one person.

"Scatterbrained kid," Darla said laughingly. "Never mind, as long as we have our costumes." She grinned at Amity and patted the bench beside her. "Have a seat. The play won't start for another thirty minutes." She gestured to a small, dark-haired, dark-eyed woman sitting beside her. "Connie tells me you're going to be our new Mary Magdalene."

"I hope so," Amity croaked, then swallowed audibly. She jumped as more people burst through the front door.

"Don't worry, they'll break you in slowly," Darla reassured her. "Just stick by me tonight and do whatever I do. You'll soon feel more comfortable."

"So Dani said," Amity replied, aware of the growing number of people, with and without costumes, who entered the room. She sat quietly and watched with interest as conversation buzzed around her.

Little children, as well as elderly men and women, sat within the group, talking and laughing until the noise threatened to deafen Amity. Various ones waved to catch her attention, then nodded and smiled before continuing their conversations. Amity relaxed a little. The people really were friendly. Besides, why was she so nervous, anyway? She had been in plenty of plays. Of course, before now she had never suspected half the people in the cast to be possible crank callers, even murderers.

The door was constantly opening with a steady stream of people going in and out. Nelson walked in, his dark brown eyes scanning the crowd until they stopped at Amity. He smiled and winked before turning away to speak to one of the apostles, then leaving again.

The noise lessened in volume when Clem entered, wearing the full, flowing robes of Pilate. Dani handed him a crown, which he settled on his head and secured with hidden combs.

"Okay, everybody, listen up." His deep voice stopped the remaining chatter.

He lifted a clipboard and waved it in front of them, glaring around the room. "I have here a list of rules you people have broken, and I dare say you know who you are." He laid the clipboard back on the counter and raised his hand pleadingly. "Remember, this play is not fun and games. It isn't just an ordinary play, but a ministry for God."

One of the apostles nudged another one, and Clem glanced at them. "Yes, Jim, your name was mentioned."

The young man ducked his head. "But it wasn't my idea to go into the director's office, it was. . .someone else's."

"Oh? And I suppose that 'someone else' had a bull ring in your nose and led you there by force?"

"It was harmless! He was only looking up a girl's name and address so he could ask her out."

"I don't suppose it would occur to him to ask her himself?"

"No, but I'll mention it to him," Jim murmured.

"You do that. Now, those of you who wear glasses: I'm sorry, I know it's hard, but we cannot allow you to wear them during your performance. As far as we know, there were no such devices in Jesus' day, so we'll wear none now. If you can't see well enough to run down the hill, I suggest you don't try it. That's tricky enough as it is."

Amity frowned and raised a hand to her stomach. That was what Dani had said. Just how dangerous was it?

"I want everyone to meet out new Mary Magdalene understudy," Clem announced, snapping Amity to attention. "This is Amity Hudson, and I trust you will all try to make her feel at ease." His dark gaze traveled around the room. "Any questions? Arguments?" There was scattered laughter, as if no one would have the audacity to argue with Clem. "Good, then I'll ask Frank to lead us in prayer."

Amity bowed her head, hiding her surprise. She knew she should have expected prayer, but this was something new to her. Never before had she worked on a stage where actors and actresses prayed before a performance. It was just one more reminder that she was not acting in a regular play, but was actually contributing to a true Christian endeavor. It comforted her.

The music that emerged from the speakers changed cadence and everyone tensed. The men who were dressed as guards trooped out of the room, followed by the rest.

"Come on," Darla called.

Amity needed no further encouragement to stick close beside Darla and Connie. The two women led the way up more stout, wooden steps, and slunk through the darkness between two concrete buildings.

"All you have to do," Darla instructed, "is walk along with me. Pretend you're buying groceries in the marketplace. Just keep a close eye on me, because Connie will get separated from us later."

They emerged from the via and Amity realized they were walking on a street of Jerusalem, headed toward the temple. She took special care not to look at the audience as she listened to Darla and Connie talk quietly.

"Here come the sheep. Don't worry, they know where they're going," Darla said.

"Yeah." Connie laughed. "The animals know their parts better than some people. And they don't break into the director's office when he's gone."

"Who was the other man with Jim?"

"I don't know, but I bet he really caught a chewing out from his manager. Clem's more lenient than most of them."

"Oh, good, here comes the sausage and cheese cart," Darla exclaimed. "Are you going to buy today?"

"No, I have to pay my taxes," Connie said. "Come up with me to the temple steps."

"No, look! Here comes Jesus!" Darla grabbed Amity by the arm. "Come on, let's go see if we can touch him!"

Amity glanced around and, sure enough, there came the actor portraying Jesus, dressed in a white robe and riding on a small donkey. Her heartbeats quickened as she allowed her friends to pull her to him.

Her breath caught in her throat. How like this it really must have been! She was living the part she played, more than she ever had before.

Then her gaze was drawn to Titus and the spell was broken. He was watching her and their gazes held for a moment before she backed into the crowd to join her friends.

The people formed a semicircle around the temple steps while Jesus and his disciples sat on the steps. As the story of the play unfolded, Amity once more pushed Titus from her mind and immersed herself in the part. The crowd, sometimes defending Jesus and sometimes condemning Jesus, seemed willing to be swayed in any direction, and Amity felt her throat constrict. This, too, must have been the way it was in Jesus' time.

In and out of scenes, up and down hills, she followed Darla, grateful she was with someone who knew where to go when. She would have been lost several times, the backstage area was so vast.

She watched Peter closely when it came time for his denial. She could see him much better from here than she had from the audience. He was so expressive that her heart constricted for him as he fled the scene of the denial, his face contorted in agony.

In the scene with Pilate, the crowd yelled, "Crucify him! Crucify him!" and Amity felt Darla nudge her. She was supposed to shout along with the rest, shaking her fist in condemnation of Jesus.

She opened her mouth, but the words would not come. *No!* her heart cried out. All her drama classes, all her plays had not prepared her to go so totally against her nature.

"Crucify him!" the crowd shouted again.

Amity watched in horror as they whipped Jesus, then laid the heavy cross on his shoulders. He stumbled beneath the load. She followed the procession up along the via.

Someone grasped her arm and she turned around to find Nelson walking alongside her. "How do you like it?" he asked, breaking the spell that had held her.

"I. . .I can't say right now. It's very real, isn't it?"

Nelson shrugged. "It's just a play."

Amity frowned at him. That was why he would never be able to take Titus's place as Peter, because to Nelson, it was only a play.

"Come on!" Darla hissed, tugging at Amity's other arm. "That was our last appearance. If we hurry and get dressed, we can sneak up behind some buildings and see the ascension."

Amity pulled away from Nelson and hurried along behind Darla to the dressing room.

"Well, how did you like it?" one of the women asked as she changed.

"It's even better close up," Amity said. "You can really get lost in it, can't you?"

"It's that way all the time. It never gets old to me," another woman said.

After they had dressed, Amity and Darla joined Dani and hurried back toward Golgotha, through dark tunnels and up the backstage stairways. When they emerged near the top of the hill, Amity could hear doves, pigeons, and chickens, some of the live props that had been used earlier in the play.

At the top of the hill, Jesus was surrounded by his disciples.

"We barely made it," Darla whispered. "Here goes."

Amity watched in fascination while Jesus was lifted up and away from the small group of disciples, just as it had happened the other night. Arms spread wide across the sky, he was spotlighted until he reached the tops of the tall oak trees. The lights then switched back down to the disciples, who bowed as the audience applauded.

No matter how thoroughly Amity searched the sky, she could not find the bright, white robe Jesus was wearing. He had disappeared completely.

Darla bid Amity and Dani good night and disappeared through one of the darkened doorways and, as she went in, Nelson came out, fully dressed.

"You two ladies look like you need an escort back to the dressing rooms. Mind if I join you?"

Dani dimpled up at him, then shot a sly glance at Amity. "We don't mind, but I need to talk to one of the apostles before he gets away. If you show Amity the way back down, I'll meet her there." With a quick smile and a wave of her hand, she ran back up into the darkness where the apostles were coming down.

"Good thing I came along, wasn't it?" Nelson said as he took Amity's arm to guide her down the concrete Via Dolorosa. "Do you have a ride home tonight? I suppose Titus is taking you."

"Yes, he is."

"Are you two pretty close friends?"

"Yes." Amity smiled. "Titus is a very good friend. We've known each other since last year."

"Is there any reason you couldn't go out with me sometime?"

Amity stopped at a familiar-looking door. "Isn't this the door that leads to the stairway?"

"Uh, yes, it is. Sorry." He pulled the heavy door open and stepped inside ahead of her. "I still get lost sometimes, even after all this time. This place can be a maze."

Amity sidestepped out of his way and preceded him down the steps toward the lighted door of Group Three. "I'll wait for Dani here, thanks."

Nelson made a wry face as he joined her at the door. "I guess that means I can't convince you to go out with me."

"I'm sorry," Amity said gently, "but I don't think so. Thank you for the compliment."

A few minutes after Nelson left, Dani arrived, her blue eyes dancing with excitement. She chattered all the way to the parking lot. There, she grew suddenly quiet, and when Amity looked up to see why, Dani's smile had slipped from her face to be replaced by a strange expression of wariness.

Titus, Clem, and Enid stood together beside Titus's Jeep. Clem's arm rested lightly across Enid's shoulders, and Dani stared hard at them.

"Enid," Clem said in an undertone that nevertheless carried to Amity and Dani, "it's so nice to come out and find you waiting for me. Do you know how many times I'd hoped you'd do this?"

"Don't let this spoil your joy," Enid said dryly, "but I came to see my niece in the play." She laughed up at him, then slanted a look toward his daughter. "Dani, you'll make a lovely Salome."

"Thanks," Dani mumbled. The lips that had smiled at Amity throughout the night now drooped in despondency.

"Come with us," Clem said, urging Enid toward a dark blue pickup truck. "Dani and I can take you home."

"No need for that," Enid said, pulling gently away from him. "Titus and Amity are going straight home."

Dani grasped her father's arm and tugged him toward the truck. "Makes perfect sense to me, Dad. Let's go, I'm tired."

"Oh, all right," Clem said, looking back at Enid with an apologetic shrug.

She smiled with false brightness. "See you in church Sunday."

"How about tomorrow night, since there's no play?" Clem suggested.

"Can't. I've got some part-time help I need to break in," Enid said. She climbed into the back seat of the Jeep.

"But Enid, I can—" Amity began, then stopped at the look on her aunt's face.

"Nope, no time. Let's go."

Titus started the Jeep, put it in gear, and drove away with a wave toward Clem, who sat watching them leave.

"Now you see what I mean?" Enid demanded. "The kid can't stand the sight of me."

Amity grabbed at her hair as it blew in the wind. "I don't understand it. She was so sweet to me all night." Amity glanced back and saw Enid's face clouded over with disappointment.

"I hardly let Clem so much as hold my hand when she's around." Enid sighed. "Danielle just doesn't want me near her father."

"So you're going to give up on Clem?" Amity asked.

Titus chuckled. "She won't give up that easily."

"I'm not playing games," Enid said. "My life is full, and I don't need this extra grief. I think Danielle's going to get her way." As soon as the Jeep stopped, she climbed out and went inside.

"We'll see about that," Titus said with a smile.

seven

The night was warm and it smelled of a thousand growing things as Amity and Titus climbed out of the Jeep.

Amity breathed deeply and strolled slowly along the sidewalk. "I don't blame Aunt Enid. Why should she throw her freedom away on a relationship that probably won't work out? So few do anymore."

"Watch it," Titus frowned at her. "You sound like a hardcore cynic. Marriage can be a wonderful relationship between two mature Christians who love each other and put God first in their lives."

"Oh, yeah? Ever been married?"

"No, but I want to be someday, naive as that may sound," he said dryly.

"Better count the cost first."

"I've counted the cost of the lonely, self-absorbed existence without a marriage blessed by God."

"Think you can do better than most?"

"God can. I saw it in my parents so I know it's possible. You weren't married long enough, or to the right person, to qualify you to judge."

"And how do you know when it's the right person? I'd probably make the same mistake again."

He stopped walking and turned to look at her in the darkness. "Amity, don't you think it's time you forgave yourself for that one mistake? It isn't as if you had blatantly disobeyed God's will. You believed Chad was a Christian."

Amity looked up into a sky that was bright with stars and held a nearly full moon. "Let's go on up this hill. This night is too beautiful to spend it arguing about marriage."

Titus agreed willingly and adjusted his long stride to hers. Amity could not help but be impressed by the difference between his presence and Chad's. With Titus she felt safe and happy. She could not remember a time when she actually felt calm and at peace with Chad.

She gazed at the thick shrubbery and trees growing around them and she smiled.

"Something funny?" Titus asked when he caught sight of her smile beneath a streetlight.

"Not really. I'm just glad I'm not as frightened as I was when I first arrived here."

"So the healing powers have already begun to work on you?"

"The what?"

"The healing powers of the valley." He slowed his steps. "The native Americans all believed that the springs down in that valley had magical healing powers." He guided her off the sidewalk onto a grassy knoll then released her to gesture toward one spring a few yards away. The little pool sparkled in the moonlight.

"Their belief was so strong," Titus continued, "that even the tribes who were hostile toward one another met here in peace, because they believed that if they fought here, the Great Spirit would become angry and dry up the springs. The Osage, who held this territory, allowed all tribes access to the healing springs."

"But the springs weren't really healing springs, were they?"

"No. They do produce some of the sweetest water in the world, but they don't have any healing powers. Neither does that statue over on Magnetic Mountain," he said, pointing toward the illuminated statue of Christ, which glowed like a beacon from the darkness of the trees surrounding it. "But it's the Spirit of Christ that heals. He heals the soul. The statue was only meant to be a reminder of His promise, of His open arms, giving the gift of life, accepting us with all our faults."

"And we have lots of those," Amity said softly.

"Emmet Sullivan knew what he was doing when he sculpted that statue. He depicted our Lord in the way I most like to think of Him. . .forgiving. So stop flogging yourself, Amity. You've repented a hundred times over. God knows it."

Amity turned and ambled back down the hill, stepping carefully on the uneven sidewalk. "I obviously was not walking as close to God as I thought I was or I would have picked up on Chad's counterfeit spirit. It's frightening to think the same thing may happen again."

"But you've learned and through it you have grown closer to God. You've seen Chad's character and you'll know what to beware of next time."

Amity grimaced. Maybe there should not be a next time.

Titus caught up with her. "In fact, I trust your judgment so much, you may well be the person to help me with my new project."

"You mean the New Holy Land?"

"No, I want to start a Christian school here in the Springs or someplace close."

"You plan to do it yourself? Is that why you left Texas to come here?"

"That was why I left my teaching job, but I didn't realize this was where I wanted to start the school until I'd been here for a while."

"You picked a good place for it. Would the children just come from Eureka Springs?"

"I hope to get them from Berryville, Green Forest, and as far away as Springdale and Fayetteville. If everything goes as I plan, we could have a boardinghouse for the kids who live too far away to commute."

"How could you pay for it?"

"My grandfather left an inheritance and my parents lived on the interest during the lean years at the mission. Now they have a church supporting them and they've decided to give the money to me. I've saved a considerable sum in the past six years and it should cover the building. What better way to invest your money than to give it to God for later returns?"

The wind chimes at The Annalee rang a greeting as Amity ran lightly up the steps beside Titus.

"Amity?" He put a hand on her arm and she turned to face him. "Are you interested?"

She took a deep breath. "Oh, I don't know. It sounds good and I love Eureka Springs, but I'm still not sure what I want to do with my life."

"I think I can understand that." He released her and dropped his hand to his side. "Right now you're in limbo. I won't push you for an answer. You have as long as you need to think it over. But keep me in mind, will you?"

"It would be hard not to."

He smiled at her, his expression tender. Those eyes, oh, those hazy, sea green eyes, they seemed to understand so much.

He raised his hand again and caressed her cheek as his gaze slowly grew serious. "You've changed a lot since last year, Amity Hudson. I know I've told you that before, but it's true. Last year I liked you a lot, but you didn't seem to know what you wanted for your life. I hate to think about what you went through after your marriage, but I like the growth I see there now."

She felt herself flush. "Thank you, Titus. I didn't do the growing, God did it for me. I was so desperate, I had to turn to God for comfort and help because I had nowhere else to turn. I'm ashamed to admit that it took that for me to get my bearings. You've always followed God, never rebelled."

"Don't believe that. Everyone has questions sometime. . . everyone rebels."

She shrugged. "Some of us more than others."

"But you aren't rebelling now."

"No, not now. The thing is, I still don't know exactly what I want for my life."

His smile returned. "Yes, you do. You want God in the center of it. After that, it's up to Him, isn't it?"

"Yes, it is. What a comfort to remember that God is in control. If only I wouldn't forget that so easily."

"I'll keep praying for you."

"Thank you," she said. "Titus, it's getting late."

"Yes." He hesitated, as if trying to make a decision. He took a deep breath. "Yes, it's late. Time for bed. But first. . ." He leaned closer to her, hesitated again, then closed his eyes and kissed her.

It was an unpracticed kiss, gentle and brief, but it was the sweetest kiss Amity had ever received.

ৡ

Later, back in the room that Enid had fixed up for her in the attic, Amity leaned against the closed door and fought sudden, overwhelming dizziness. The niggling suspicions of the past few weeks once again weighed on her. The dizziness. . . the nausea. . .

Stress. Had to be stress. Stress caused symptoms like these. Anything else was unthinkable at this point.

She buried her face in her hands and fought the quick tears that sprang to her eyes. "Oh, God, help me," she whispered. "Please, help me."

Her prayers continued silently throughout the next two weeks, and although Opal Shrum's presence freed her for more time to practice her part, she seriously considered quitting the play.

Sunday morning Amity awoke to the whistling sound of the wind and the lonely echo of a chain tapping a metal flagpole somewhere in the neighborhood. The sky did not glow with its usual warmth, but glared down coldly.

In spite of the dreariness of the day, Amity's continuous prayers and closeness to God gave her a sense of peace. God would not leave her alone.

She stretched her arms high above her head, yawned, and

pulled herself out from under the covers to walk across to the window and get a better look at the weather.

Sure enough, the sky was leaden and morose and wind whipped the tree branches to and fro. Two unhappy robins clung precariously to a branch by her window.

She turned to gaze contentedly at her shadowed room. It was an attic room but it had a special charm. After all, the one little window in it overlooked the valley she had come to love. Though the room lacked the elegant Victorian furniture that graced the rest of the house, Amity still loved its cozy seclusion.

Within thirty minutes she had washed and descended to the first floor, ready for church in a loose-fitting dress of red gauze. Her water-darkened hair trailed in a straight line to the middle of her back, and she tucked a few damp tendrils behind her ear as she walked toward the kitchen. The sudden trilling of the telephone rerouted her, and she stepped into the sitting room to answer it.

"Hello, this is The Annalee. May I help you?"

No one answered but Amity heard soft breathing at the other end of the line and a prickling of old fear coursed up her spine.

"H–hello, who's there?"

The line went dead.

Amity's fingers went numb and she dropped the receiver. "Not again!" she whispered.

"Amity?" Titus's deep voice came from the doorway. "What's wrong?" He crossed to her side and touched her shoulder. "What happened?"

"The phone rang," she said, her voice shaking. "When I answered, they held for a moment, then hung up. Oh, Titus, what if it's them? They've found me!"

He put his arm around her shoulders and drew her closer. "Don't panic. You're safe here. I'm not going to let anything happen to you. You didn't identify yourself, did you?"

"No." She wanted to believe him, she really did. "I hate being so afraid."

"I know, Amity. I'm sorry. I wish Farris would contact the police."

"Why hasn't she?" Amity asked in frustration.

"I don't know. I don't understand her reasoning, but don't forget that I'm here. I'll do everything in my power to keep you safe. Remember that you are in God's hands, though. He is watching over you and protecting you."

His assurance and closeness strengthened her and she felt as if he had lifted a weight from her shoulders. She had come to depend on him more and more, but with their growing friendship she had developed some misgivings. Was he expecting more from her than friendship? She did not have more to offer . . .did she? Was she being fair to him? She had to admit to herself that if the situation were different, she might easily fall in love with Titus King and it would be a love that would last. But right now those thoughts were counterproductive.

The wind picked up velocity, ringing the chimes more loudly. Amity glanced outside. "Do you think we should bring those things in? They sound like they're about to be bashed to pieces against the side of the house."

"They'll be okay."

She turned back to find his gaze riveted on her.

"Your hair's wet," he observed, lifting a strand to trail it idly through his fingers. He held it up and inhaled its soft scent. "Smells wonderful."

Her heart once more began its erratic pounding. Even the timbre of his voice sent shivers of excitement through her. But with it rose a cautioning voice in her mind, and she drew back from him. "I think I'll help Enid with breakfast," she said quickly.

"Okay, Amity." His voice held a note of a question in it, and a hint of disappointment.

She hesitated. "Titus, you're such a good friend, maybe just about my best friend, and. . ."

"Yes?"

"And I need a good friend right now. That's what I need. . . a friend."

His gaze did not leave her face. "Is this one of those 'Dear John' scenes where the lady wants to let the gentleman down gently, so she says, 'We can always be friends'?"

"No, Titus, it isn't. It's one of those scenes where the confused lady doesn't know exactly what's going on in her heart right now, but she does know she desperately needs the gentleman's friendship and understanding."

"Since the gentleman is sure about what's going on in his own heart, and since he trusts God, he will wait."

"Thanks, Titus." She reached up and kissed his cheek and then went into the kitchen.

"Good morning, sunshine!" Enid greeted as she turned sausage patties in the skillet. "Looks like you'll be the only sunshine today. Storm's brewing, I believe."

Amity dug through the linen drawer and pulled out an apron. "What will rain do to the play tonight?"

"That depends on the severity of the storm. Unless it just pours down, or hails, or worse, the show will go on."

"You mean they have it in the rain?" Amity tied the apron around her waist, but not too tightly. "I bet that's a mess."

"Oh, they handle the rain quite nicely," Enid assured her, draining the sausage on paper towels and slicing more to fry. "It's the hail that really gets them. That can really get wild! Last year, a young couple from my old church got caught in the hail."

Amity stacked dishes and glasses on the table and measured coffee into the pot. "Sounds dangerous."

"It could be, but it rarely happens."

"Speaking of church, didn't you say Clem and Dani belonged to yours?"

"Please! I'm trying to forget," Enid protested. "Isn't Farris supposed to soar back to town on her broomstick soon?"

"This afternoon sometime. And she's coming in my BMW. The trees are too thick for a broomstick."

The sausage sizzled in the skillet, sending the smoky aroma through the kitchen once more. Amity's stomach complained with hunger, and she pilfered a cooked piece from the serving plate.

"If you have to steal me blind, at least do it behind my back," Enid teased. "You're making me hungry, and I can't eat breakfast this morning. Our choir is singing a special at church."

Amity poured a glass of orange juice and set it on the counter in front of her aunt. "This won't hurt. Have you ever tried talking to Dani alone?"

"Uh-oh, here we go again," Enid muttered. "No, the girl won't even let me close enough. She must think I have leprosy."

Amity regarded her aunt thoughtfully and said no more. But she knew that if Dani only got to know Enid well that things would work out. No one could resist Enid for long. Perhaps a little talk with Dani. . .

"Mmmm, smells delicious," Titus said from the doorway. His smiling eyes lingered on Amity a moment before he glanced at Enid. "I see our hostess is on her usual Sunday morning fast, sitting in the corner, drinking orange juice and coffee."

"It's a juice fast," Enid said. She tossed her head. "Lots of people do it."

For the past three Sundays, Amity had stayed and watched the lodge while Enid and Titus attended church, and she was looking forward to going today. She ate quickly and urged her aunt to hurry and get dressed so they would get there early. While she and Titus waited for Enid in the sitting room, Amity fidgeted nervously.

"Now what's wrong?" Titus asked. "You're still as frightened as a caged wild rabbit."

Amity put a hand to her stomach and sat down.

Just then the kitchen door swung open, and they turned to

see Opal come in with a dust cloth in her hand. "Good morning," she said as she set to work on the coffee table. "Sorry if I'm intruding but I've found that if I get my work done early, I have the rest of the day to sightsee."

"We should be back a little after noon," Amity said. "Will that be soon enough?"

"Oh, sure," Opal said. "I have enough laundry to keep me busy until then." She smiled at Amity, finished her dusting, and left.

A strong gust of wind broke off small limbs and leaves outside, and the sky darkened even more. Amity shivered and paced the room.

"You sure we should be taking your Jeep?" she asked Titus.

"Why not?"

"What if it rains before we get home?" she asked.

"What if it does?"

"Won't we get a little wet riding with the top down?"

"Better get used to it. We might have to play in the rain tonight," he teased, then sobered. "Amity, that isn't what's bothering you. I've told you not to worry about the phone call."

"Yes. . .well. . .I could lie and tell you I'm not, but. . ." She shrugged expressively.

Enid called from the hallway. "Let's get a move on or we'll be late!"

Amity glanced up, then gasped appreciatively as Enid stepped into the room. "Wow! You look beautiful."

Wearing a tailored black skirt and jacket, Enid had expressed her fragile femininity with a lacy red blouse with a neckline that encircled her throat and framed her face like a flower.

"Honey, you do wonders for the ego," she said as they followed Titus out to the Jeep.

The car, to Amity's surprise, was covered by a soft top, and she chuckled when Titus took her arm to help her in. "You couldn't tell me, could you? You had to tease."

"I wasn't teasing about the fact that we really may have to play in the rain tonight."

"The show must go on," Enid said as she climbed into the backseat. "Just be glad they don't continue the play through the winter. I can imagine how warm those sandals would keep your feet in the snow and ice."

"Yes, and I'd pity the people who had to run up and down the icy hill," Amity said. Again she thought of her part as Mary, and she automatically put a gentle hand on her stomach.

The gray clouds overhead raced across the sky and Amity could see rain falling in the distance, but it was so far away she doubted it would reach them. She had been in Eureka Springs long enough to know that when it rained in one field, it did not necessarily rain in the one next to it. She sat watching the clouds as Titus turned the Jeep out of town along the highway.

They went several miles before Titus turned off the road onto a narrow, rough gravel path, hedged with trees. Mist rose from the cool green of the forest, creating an ethereal beauty in the dim light. A lone meadowlark warbled from some hidden fencepost, and Amity searched for the bright yellow of its breast among the trees.

The steepening road plunged them down into a tiny valley and the forest suddenly drew back from them, revealing the lighter green of a grassy hillock. On its crest stood a small white church house. A long, narrow lake below reflected a leaden sky, and several small children played on a footbridge that crossed the lake at its narrowest point.

Clem stepped out of the church and reached the Jeep quickly, his dark eyes fixed on Enid's face with determination. He stood, unsmiling, while they all got out.

"Good morning Amity, Titus." He nodded toward them but his attention was on Enid.

"Good morning, Clem. Where's Dani today?" Amity glanced again at her aunt, whose face had darkened to a scowl.

"She went on inside." Clem finally looked at Amity. "She'll be glad to see you. She was wondering if you would come." He looked back at Enid. "How about a walk down by the lake? The pastor isn't here yet, so we'll have time before church starts."

Titus took Amity by the arm and led her toward the building. "Can't you see your aunt wants to be alone right now?"

"Oh? By the look on her face, she'd sooner be swimming in a pit of copperheads."

Though small, the room was larger than it had appeared from the outside, and its simplicity was refreshing. Two of the windows were cracked open to let in a draft of the sweet-smelling air. Wooden benches, their seats comfortably padded, were divided into three sections across the room and were attached to a well-preserved, hardwood floor. The pulpit and communion table were plain and square, just like the pews in the choir section.

"No wonder Enid was concerned about her voice," Amity commented. "There can't be room for more than seven people in the choir."

"There's no more than that in the choir," Titus said dryly. "It's a small church."

"Amity!" A youthful, lilting voice called to her from a side aisle, and Amity turned to see Dani, weaving her way through pews and people. "I was hoping you'd come," the teenager said, smiling at her. "Hi, Titus," Dani said as she came up behind Amity. "Do you two want to sit with me this morning? I promise not to sit in the front row."

"In that case, I'd love to," Amity said.

"Lead on," Titus said.

True to her word, Dani did not sit in front, but in the back row, chattering excitedly while they waited for the services to begin. "Didn't you love the play last night? Mary Magdalene almost fell again. I think it's the sandals she wears. Don't you think the man who plays Jesus is great? But wait until you see his understudy. He's gorgeous!"

"Was he the one you went to talk to the other night?" Amity asked.

Dani grinned broadly. "That's the one. Did you see him?"

"No. Nelson was busy trying to find the right door. I'll have to pay special attention tonight."

"If it doesn't storm too badly. I hope it doesn't. Our neighbors have hay down, and I—" Dani abruptly fell silent.

Amity glanced up at her and saw the girl's eyes. In through the back door came Enid and Clem, deep in conversation, their heads close together. The scowl had vanished from Enid's face.

Amity looked up at Titus, who was watching her with amusement. "What did I tell you?" he said.

Amity nodded and then darted a glance at Dani's unhappy expression. After church, maybe the two of them could have a talk.

The service began soon, much to Amity's relief, and Dani did not utter another word. She just sat watching her father and Enid, her eyes mirroring a mixture of hurt and, Amity could have sworn, fear.

The weather continued to threaten and complain throughout the service, but did little to distract the worshippers from singing, praying, and listening with rapt attention to the excellent speaker. Uplifted by this little church and the honest faith of its believers, Amity was sorry when the service concluded.

Many people rushed up to greet Amity after the service, and it was several moments before she realized that Dani had disappeared. Scanning the crowd, she saw Enid and Clem talking in the corner with Titus, but Dani was nowhere in the church.

Then Amity spied her. Down by the lake, her shining blond hair blowing around her like a cloud in the wind, Dani walked alongside the water, her head bent.

Amity slipped out the door and strolled down the hill

toward her. Few birds were out today and the spring green usually so bright, had been tamed by the gray of the clouds Still, the breeze carried with it a magical fragrance and the beauty of the little valley assaulted Amity's senses, as Eureka Springs had done since she had arrived.

Dani spared a glance and a quick smile as Amity approached, then resumed her intense contemplation of the water. Amity fell into step beside her, grasping at her own hair, which the wind whipped in all directions.

"Does it often do this around here?" Amity asked.

Dani nodded and looked up at the sky. "It rains a lot, but that's why it's so beautiful. Water, water, everywhere. From springs to rivers to lakes, but especially from the rain. I think I like the rainy days best."

"Especially when you're so gloomy yourself."

Dani jerked dark blue eyes toward Amity. "I don't mean to be."

Amity chuckled and tugged a long strand of Dani's blond hair. "Everyone gets that way sometimes."

"If I tell you something, will you promise not to get mad?"

"Okay, I promise."

"I. . .I called The Annalee this morning. I know I should have said something, but—"

"You!" Amity stopped and stared at the girl. "It was you?"

"Yes, but you promised not to get mad."

Amity felt herself go weak with relief. "I'm not mad. Why didn't you talk to me?"

"I'm sorry, I really am. I was calling to talk to Enid, but I chickened out. I couldn't think of anything to say to you. You won't tell her, will you?" She laid a hand of entreaty on Amity's arm.

"Why should I tell her? Are you going to tell me why you called?"

Dani pursed her lips and shook her head.

"Dani, why don't you like my aunt?"

Dani shrugged and ducked her head.

Amity tried again. "Why don't you just give her a chance? She doesn't want to take your father away from you, she wants to be friends with you."

Dani raised a suspicious brow. "I've heard that before."

"You mean you've chased other women away from your dad?" Amity asked bluntly.

Dani tossed her head with irritation. "Why is it so many women think they have to take this poor little motherless child under their wings? They don't, you know." She swung around to face Amity. "Ask Dad. He'll tell you, himself, how much better life has been since my precious mother died! And he doesn't even know the whole story!"

Amity made a valiant attempt to hide her shock. She cleared her throat and stepped onto the bridge. "I suppose this is safe?" At Dani's nod, she stepped gingerly onto the wooden planking, glad for the excuse for a pause.

Dani followed, and their footsteps echoed hollowly beneath the curved bridge.

"Tell me about your mother," Amity said. She stopped to lean against the wooden railing and gaze into the lake. The dark green mountains engulfed the valley, shadowing the water. As Amity and Dani looked down, their reflections flickered up darkly against the mirrored gray of the sky.

"I'd rather tell you about my father," Dani said, her eyes softening with affection. "He's the one who loved me. My mother never wanted me in the first place." Some of the youthfulness disappeared from her face. "One time, Mother had some friends visiting. I guess I was about nine at the time." She turned to face Amity.

"Mother thought I was out in the hay field with Dad. . .I spent a lot of time with him. . .but this time I was in my room, reading. I could hear the conversation in the other room, but I didn't really pay much attention to it until they started arguing about abortion. The other women didn't believe in it, I could tell, and Mother got mad and announced that she'd just recently had an abortion and that she wished she'd had one when she was carrying me, too." Dani's eyes clouded with tears, and she swallowed hard, her chin quivering. She looked up at Amity. "She never even told Dad she'd had the abortion. Before I could slip out the door, she caught me. She threatened me, and made me promise not to tell Dad."

"Did you ever?"

"No, I never have." Dani sniffed and blotted her face with the wide collar of her dress. "Why hurt him? Mother had done enough of that already. He was so good to her, but she was never satisfied. And you should have seen her when he paid special attention to me!" She laughed bitterly. "She was like a cat with her claws bared, although why she was jealous, I don't know. She didn't love Dad. She just married him because he had money. I heard her tell her friends that, too." She bit her trembling lower lip. "My own mother wished I'd never been born."

"Your dad is glad you were."

"Dad wasn't around then. He married my mother after I was born, then adopted me." Dani smiled. "I used to pretend that he married Mother just because he wanted me to be his daughter."

Amity put a comforting hand on Dani's shoulders. "That could have been true, you know."

A footfall on the bridge startled them. "Are you two just standing out here, daring the rain to fall?" Titus asked.

"We just thought we'd get some practice for tonight," Amity said with a grin. She glanced at Dani. "I think he's ready to go. Want to walk back up with us?"

Dani's gaze traveled up the hill to Clem and Enid, standing together beside the Jeep. "I think I'll wait."

"Okay," Amity said. "But will you just give her one little chance? She won't let you down."

"I'll think about it," Dani said grudgingly, then left them and walked across the bridge to the far side of the lake.

"Do I detect a little friendly interference?" Titus asked as they walked side by side in the ankle-deep grass toward the Jeep.

"It couldn't hurt, could it?"

"No, but if you're passing out advice, maybe you'd be open to some, too."

"For instance?"

"What you told Dani will do for starters. Give others a chance. Don't presume that just because Chad turned out to be false, the rest of us are, too."

Amity looked up at Titus, at the tenderness in his expression, at the warmth in his eyes, and her throat constricted at the sight of him.

"Oh, Titus, there's nothing false about you. I hope you don't think I'm comparing you to him. He was an abuser. You're one of the kindest, most thoughtful men I've ever known. You deserve the very best life has to offer."

"Aha! So I've got you fooled."

"Titus, I think you're blushing."

He sobered and held her gaze. "Thank you, Amity." He touched her arm and slowed her stride to point out across the valley. "What do you think? Would this be a good place for our school?"

"What do you mean 'our school'? I haven't even told you if I'm interested."

"But you are, aren't you?"

She quickened her steps as they neared the Jeep. "Okay, okay, I'm interested, but only if that doesn't mean committed."

"Good. We'll go over some of the plans this afternoon." He hesitated then quirked a brow at her. "If that's okay with you."

Amity chuckled as they reached the Jeep. "You'd make a good bulldozer."

eight

Amity's stomach rolled sickeningly as the Jeep climbed the steep, rough road out of the valley. A thin film of perspiration formed on her upper lip and forehead. Enid had been right when she said this humid atmosphere took some getting used to. It was probably preparing to rain and the air was extra-heavy just now.

Her stomach rolled again when they hit another rough bump. If only she could hold out until they reached the highway.

"Amity?" Enid reached forward to touch her niece's arm. "Honey, are you okay? Your face is ashen!" She pressed a gentle hand against Amity's damp, clammy forehead.

"Motion sickness," Amity assured her. "Titus, may I suggest blacktopping this road before building the school? This ride would frighten all the students away, and if not them, their parents."

"That was one of my first decisions," he said. "I'll tell you about the rest this afternoon."

"School?" Enid asked. "What school are you talking about?" She fixed a stern look on Titus. "What haven't you told me?"

He grinned. "Well, if you must know, I've been talking to Amity about some dreams I have about starting a Christian school in this valley." He explained more about it, while Amity tried to take shallow, deep breaths and think of peaceful, serene thoughts that would not upset her stomach anymore.

"You're planning to have a boarding school?" Enid asked. "Who would run it?"

"Now, Enid," Titus warned. "I see that gleam in your eyes. This won't be for quite some time yet. Anything can happen.

You may have someone else to think about by then."

"Don't count on it."

"You mean you and Clem haven't reached a truce yet?"

"Clem isn't the only one involved in this." She shook her head. "I'm not even sure I'm involved, or want to be. But the school sounds wonderful."

Amity leaned back with relief when she felt the smooth road beneath them. When they reached the house, Titus left the two women downstairs and went up to change.

"I'll see what Opal's up to," Enid said, stepping toward the kitchen.

Amity followed, and they entered a clean, thoroughly scrubbed kitchen, with the aroma of baking ham wafting through the air.

"Opal's probably upstairs getting ready to go out," Amity said. "I think she wanted to go sightseeing this afternoon."

"Oh?" Enid tied on her apron and opened a cupboard door. "I thought she was meeting a friend for lunch downtown."

"Maybe they're both going sightseeing."

As they talked, Opal burst into the room, her short, light brown hair disheveled. Her eyes widened when she saw Amity.

"Oh, there you are, Opal," Enid said. "Are you planning to eat with us?"

Opal looked dazedly out the window, then at Enid. "Pardon? Eat? N–no, I can't. I have to leave." She looked back out the window distractedly. "Is it going to storm?"

"Looks like it."

"I hate driving in storms."

Enid set down a plate. "Then why go out in it?"

"I have to. I'm supposed to meet an acquaintance at the yogurt shop. You don't need me for anything, do you?"

"No, but if you're really that frightened of storms, I'll be glad to drive you."

"No. No, that's okay. Thanks for the offer, but it's only a few blocks." Opal combed her fingers through her hair, glanced once more at Amity, then turned and walked out.

Amity frowned as she tied on her apron and filled glasses with iced tea. "I know how Opal feels. I tend to be nervous of lightning and thunder myself."

As if in reply to her words, a streak of jagged lightning flashed outside her window, followed by a loud clap of thunder.

"Then hold on tight," Enid said, "because it looks like we're in for a good display."

Titus came in, clad in a burgundy cotton pullover and a pair of white jeans. He took a deep whiff of the baking ham. "Mmm, smells great. Don't open the windows and let the aroma out or the neighbors might all decide to come for dinner. Anything I can do to help?"

Enid beamed up at him. "Amity, tell me, just how many men do you know who would walk into a kitchen and offer to help?"

Amity laid out the napkins. "Don't let him fool you. It's only because he's hungry and in a hurry to get the food on the table, isn't that right, Titus?"

"You think you know me pretty well, don't you?" Titus grinned and shrugged. "Ham is my favorite. Do we have any sweet potatoes to go with it?"

Enid took a set of pot holders, opened the oven door, and lifted out a steaming dish. "We certainly do. And a broccoli and cauliflower salad, with my special homemade mayonnaise, so I hope you have a good appetite."

Another bolt of lightning lit the sky, followed by a louder crack of thunder than last time. The lights flickered, went out, then came back on.

"Let's eat while we still have light to see by," Amity suggested, and the three of them sat down to ask the blessing.

Halfway through the meal, a deafening thunderclap startled Amity so badly she dropped her fork. Once again, the lights flickered, and this time they went out for good. Amity looked at Titus and Enid.

Titus placed his napkin on the table and stood. "I have a battery-operated radio in my room. I think I'll check out the weather, just to make sure we're not in for worse."

As he walked out, Enid leaned forward and put a hand on Amity's arm. "Is it just the dim light in here, or are you pale? Did that startle you, honey?"

"Only for a moment. I'm okay now."

Enid picked up her glass, hesitated, then put it back down again. "I saw you talking to Dani down by the lake today."

Amity picked up her fork and toyed with a broccoli spear. "We've become pretty good friends in the past few days."

"You haven't. . .mentioned me in your conversation, have you?"

"Yes, your name did come up today."

Enid's straight, black brows drew together in thought. "When I first started going to church out there, almost a year ago, Dani was the most friendly, welcoming person there. She even made it a habit of sitting with me before I joined the choir." She sighed. "There weren't many young people her age there, and I suppose she felt drawn to me for some reason, just as I was drawn to her."

"Of course," Amity said with affection. "It's your eternal youthfulness."

"Whatever it was," Enid said dryly, "her friendliness decreased in direct proportion to Clem's growing interest in me."

"Just give Dani more time, be more understanding, and let her get to really know you before you give up completely."

"We'll see."

"Really, Aunt Enid, there's a lot more to her than you think."

"Oh, I know she's a special young girl. She's got a lot going for her, but that doesn't change how she feels about me."

"It isn't you, Aunt Enid. Just give her time. Trust me."

Enid held her serious gaze for a moment. "Okay, I'll give it some time, but don't make the same mistake your parents made with you and Titus last fall. Don't try to rush things for me, okay?"

"Okay."

Titus stepped back in from the hallway, his face pale beneath its tan. His jaw muscles flexed and relaxed, flexed and relaxed.

"What's happened?" Amity asked.

He stepped toward her. "There's been an accident. Farris ran off the road over a steep embankment in the hills between here and Gateway on Highway 62."

Amity felt the blood drain from her face. "Is she okay?"

"She's alive, but unconscious. I heard the announcement over the radio and called the police."

Amity stood to her feet. "How did it happen?"

"They said it was an accident, that she must have lost control of the car in the storm. They've already contacted her uncle in Oklahoma City. At first they thought it was you, since she was in your car."

"Do they know how bad she is?"

"Not yet."

After lunch they put a call through to Farris's Uncle Jim. His housekeeper answered and Amity discovered from her that Farris had regained consciousness. With relief, Amity asked about the accident but discovered that Farris had selective amnesia and was still in the hospital.

When Amity hung up, Titus glanced up at her from the paperwork he had spread out on the sitting room coffee table. "Well?" he asked.

Amity stood up and walked restlessly to the window. "At least she's okay, but she doesn't remember anything about it." She gazed out over the drenched hillside. Leaves dripped and wind whipped the branches to and fro. "I suppose she could have skidded on the wet pavement, maybe lost control."

"Yes, she could have." He watched Amity pace. "It could have been an accident."

"You don't believe that, do you?"

"I'm not sure what to believe right now," he said. "I just want us to be careful, in case it wasn't an accident, and. . ."

"And in case someone thought I was in the car instead of Farris?"

"Yes."

Overnight boarders rang the service bell out in the hallway, and Amity could hear Enid coming down the stairs to greet them and show them to their rooms.

"There's a bathroom just one door down from you," she said as she climbed the steps ahead of them. "Breakfast is any time between seven and eleven o'clock. . ." Her voice trailed off with the diminishing footsteps and, except for the muffled sounds on the second floor, it grew quiet once again.

A car pulled along the curb outside, and Amity recognized it as Opal's elderly Chevrolet. Opal climbed out and dashed through the blowing rain to the front porch. The door stood open and she stomped energetically on the welcome mat before coming inside.

"Hello," Amity called from the sitting room. "Did you and your friend get drenched?"

Opal shook drops of water from her hair. "I did, but my friend never showed up." She waved at them and climbed the stairs.

"What a rotten thing to do, especially since Opal doesn't like storms," Amity said. "Her friend could have called to let her know she wasn't coming."

Titus got up and closed the tall sitting room doors. He turned a latch that locked them and walked back to sit down on the sofa.

"Amity, I don't want to alarm you, but have you noticed anything missing from your room?"

"What do you mean?"

He took a deep breath and leaned back. "Maybe nothing. Maybe your fear is contagious, but when I came upstairs to find my radio, it was in a different place from where I had left it. I'm not the best housekeeper in the world, but I remember where I had put the radio the last time I had it, because I kept it away from the walls so the music wouldn't disturb anyone."

"Did you notice anything else rearranged?"

"No, but as I said, I'm not the best housekeeper. Let's just keep our eyes open for the next few days. Could be one of the guests was just curious."

"But you keep your door locked, don't you?"

"Yes, and no one else is supposed to come into my room, since I clean it myself."

"Then how could another guest get in?"

"Good question. Normally it would be too small an incident to consider, but I don't want to take any chances with you."

"Are you thinking what I'm thinking? Opal sure showed up at an interesting time. She has access to the rooms."

"Yes, she does," Titus said. "I think I'll keep a closer watch on her for the next few days. We might be jumping to incorrect conclusions, but as I said—"

"You don't want to take chances. Thanks, Titus."

The hallway echoed with the tramping feet of new lodgers. Amity glanced outside to find blue sky peeping out from behind silver, gray, and white clouds, framed in the window amidst the green bush surrounding it.

"Look." She pointed toward the small patch of bright azure. "We'll have the play, after all."

Titus surveyed her expression. "Are you worried?"

"Not about the play."

"Just remember that you're safer in a crowd than you are alone. Don't allow yourself to be alone, ever. Stay beside me or with some of the other actors. Even here, I think it would be a good idea if you stayed with Enid or me."

"And endanger you?"

"If there is someone trying to get to you, they'll wait until you're alone. And if they're true to pattern, they'll try to disguise their actions. Like they did when they killed Chad."

Amity stared at him. "And tried to kill Farris?"

"Maybe."

Another thought occurred to her. She took a deep breath. "Titus, is there anyone else who could do Mary Magdalene?"

He raised a brow in surprise. "I don't believe what I'm hearing."

"I'm serious."

"I'm sure others could do it, but the directors picked you because they felt you were the best for the part. You'll be safe at the play as long as you stay with the others."

"It isn't that."

Titus frowned. "Then what?"

Amity slumped against the sofa cushions. Now what should she tell him?

"I saw how much running she had to do. In the last scene, she has to run up and down that hill several times. I know I would fall, running in those sandals."

"Try another excuse. That one won't work."

She stood and walked to the doors before turning back to him. She did not meet his eyes. "I think I'll go have a rest before dinner. Opal's back, so Enid won't need me." She unlocked the doors and stepped into the hallway, aware that Titus was watching her with puzzlement.

Her eyes felt gritty, her limbs heavy, as she climbed the long, steep steps to her attic room. Once she reached it she locked the door behind her. Would she ever feel completely safe again?

She crossed over to her dresser mirror and studied the faint darkness of skin around her eyes. Were those circles, almost permanent now, caused by fear, or by pregnancy?

She backed away and turned sideways to study the reflection of her tummy. No physical signs. But how much longer could she wait? She should see a doctor to start prenatal care.

She should have done so long before now. She had to decide whether to keep the Mary Magdalene part or to give it up. It was not fair to wait.

"Dear God," she whispered, slumping onto the edge of her bed, "please help me through this."

nine

By Sunday evening the sun shone brightly and the clouds had all but disappeared. The few small ones that lingered curved in ineffectual, puffy mist high in the sky and offered no threat.

Amity strolled along the sidewalk, deep in thought. Tourists ambled everywhere and she felt safe since half the neighbors puttered and visited out in their yards, enjoying the sunshine.

The trees dripped with water, and Amity could almost have imagined it was raining. Every time a zephyr whispered through them, their leaves lost some of their droplets, scattering them across Amity's hair and shoulders. A faint mist rose from the earth, where the sun beat down.

Amity inhaled the fresh-washed fragrance of the Springs, wondering idly if heaven smelled like this. The heavy humidity had been chased away for once and the gentle breeze felt wonderful. A lone train whistle echoed through the valley and the clanging bells of a trolley car jangled from a few blocks away.

Amity shivered. She had wandered farther than she had intended and she turned back toward the house. How long would she have to be careful like this? How long would she automatically suspect strangers and fear their actions?

Speeding up her steps, she waved as the trolley car rumbled past on the street. Several of the passengers waved back. Summer edged closer and tourists filled Eureka Springs.

Many of those people would visit the play tonight. Tonight. She would speak to Clem about finding another Mary Magdalene. Maybe he would take her more seriously than

Titus had. Of course, it would help if they knew why she was quitting, but she was not ready to talk about it yet. It was so extremely personal.

Her stomach complained of hunger, and she was glad when The Annalee came into sight. Titus had just come out the door when she walked across the flagstone sidewalk and he stood waiting for her to reach the porch.

"Why the gloomy expression?" he asked, his eyes noting the drooping corners of her mouth and her solemn gaze. "And why are you out here alone? I thought I told you to stay close to me or Enid."

"That's why the gloomy expression," she said.

"Thanks. I didn't realize my company was that depressing to you."

Amity's lips curved in a reluctant smile. "Sorry. I think I'm really just hungry."

"It's waiting for you. Come in." He held the door open as she stepped through it.

The crunchy chef salad—lettuce and cabbage tossed with chunks of their noonday ham and strips of cheese—would have gone perfectly with the cubes of garlic toast, but Amity discovered that, when she smelled the garlic, her stomach churned. Then the whole room took on the aroma of garlic and she quickly lost her appetite.

Enid gestured toward Amity's barely touched plate. "That's why you're not feeling well. You're not eating enough lately to feed a robin." She studied Amity's face worriedly and laid a hand on her niece's arm. "Honey, you can't let those people do this to you. You'll be your own worst enemy."

Amity picked up her fork and tried to choke down another mouthful. She laid the fork back down and stood to her feet. The harder she tried to eat the more ill she felt.

"I'll just go get ready for the play," she said, fleeing the room before anyone could stop her.

As she dashed through the swinging doors, she nearly

collided with Opal. "Oh, I'm sorry, Opal!" she said, then frowned and glanced back at her aunt. What was Opal doing out here in the hallway, just standing? "If you're hungry, there's a chef salad and plenty left over since I didn't eat."

"Oh no, no thanks. I was just going to the laundry room for sheets." The woman stepped through the doorway. "Thanks just the same."

Amity stood watching the dining room doors swing shut behind Opal. The woman did seem to have a knack for turning up at odd times.

Upstairs, Amity lay across the bed and stared at the ceiling. Automatically, she placed a hand across her stomach, and her eyes glowed with a dreadful, yet hopeful, knowledge. A baby. . .

A nasty voice inside her head reminded her it was Chad's baby and that it would always be a part of Chad, the man who had hurt her, beat her, and was still reaching to her from the grave to put her in danger.

She shook her head and turned onto her side. No, the baby was an individual.

She pushed from her mind, for just a moment, the problems and heartaches a baby would bring her as a single mom, and the glow within her felt soft and tender. A baby. . .

❧

That evening, after Titus walked with Amity to her group room backstage, Clem called to her from the costume counter. "I see we haven't frightened you away yet." His wide grin was warm and welcoming and made what she had to say even harder.

"No. . ." she hesitated. "Except. . ."

His smile disappeared. "Except what, Amity?"

"Oh, I hate doing this to you, but I was wondering. . .don't you think Dani would make a good Mary Magdalene? The Salome part won't be open for several more weeks." She held her breath while Clem narrowed his eyes and stared at her.

"She's not bad," he answered slowly. "But we have reason

to believe Mary might have been a little older than fifteen."

"Of course," Amity said. "But no one knows for sure, and besides, no one in the audience can tell how old Dani is from where they sit."

Clem's dark gaze never moved from Amity's face as he stepped around the counter and took her arm in a gentle grip.

"Come with me outside."

She went willingly, but was unable to stop her stomach from tightening with nerves. More explanations, when she was still unprepared to give the real reasons for her change of heart.

"Now," Clem said as they strolled away from the crowd toward the cast parking lot, "tell me what this is all about. What's bothering you, Amity? I thought you really wanted the part."

"I do." She stepped around a pile of gravel used to repair the street on the set. "But I feel guilty, snatching the part out from under Dani's nose when I know she wanted it."

Clem shook his dark head. "Dani didn't necessarily have the part, even before you tried out."

"Why not? I've seen her and she's good."

"There's the thing about her age." Clem's eyes lit with fond amusement. "She's also scatterbrained sometimes. She has the tendency to turn the wrong way or say the wrong thing at the wrong time. Especially when there's a good-looking young man around. She needs to mature. One of the other women may have gotten the part if you hadn't come along." He grinned down at her. "So that's part of your reasoning shot down. If you're anything like your dear aunt, I'm sure you must have a few more arguments. I think she said it runs in the family."

Silently, Amity wondered how her aunt could reject this attractive man. He was so handsome, his manner so confident and solid. . .so dependable. For one crazy moment, Amity considered confiding in him, but caught herself. Not yet.

"I heard this part could be dangerous," she said. "I have a phobia about falling."

"Falling?" His heavy, black brows came together to form an unbroken line across his forehead.

"You know," Amity said, "down the hill. Dani said something the other night about how easy it is to fall while running down the Via Dolorosa. I think she said she had fallen once or twice herself."

Clem threw his head back and roared with laughter. The whole parking lot echoed with the sound, startling two sheep on the hillside and causing two camels to turn their heads curiously in Clem's direction.

"That daughter of mine," he said, still chuckling. "As I said, she's a bit scatterbrained. Oh, I know it's just adolescent awkwardness and she'll outgrow it, but I don't doubt she fell more than once on that sidewalk." He sobered and looked at Amity. "You won't, though, if that's what's really bothering you. I've watched you moving on the set, it's a part of my job, and you're as graceful as a gazelle. It was one of the reasons the directors chose you for the part. You can put your fears to rest."

Instead of ending the conversation and walking back toward the dressing rooms, he continued to walk around the perimeter of parked cars, alongside the woods, and Amity went with him.

"I'm glad to see you and Titus becoming such good friends," he said. "He's been much more outgoing, less introspective since you showed up." He smiled at Amity. "You're good for him."

She glanced at Clem in surprise. "Introspective? Titus?"

Clem's smile widened. "Hard to believe, huh? Oh, I'm not saying he's been antisocial—far from it. He's made a lot of friends since he came here to Eureka Springs. But there's just been this sense of. . .oh, I don't know. . .I'd say loneliness about him. Guess I didn't really put a name to it until you showed up, and it gradually disappeared. He thinks a lot of you, Amity."

She glanced at Clem, then away. His words warmed her even as they made her sad. How could she encourage Titus this way? She was being unfair, to him as well as to herself.

"Amity? Have I spoken out of turn? I don't mean to meddle or matchmake, just state a fact."

She smiled at Clem. "I know. I think a lot of Titus, too. He's one of the kindest men I've ever known. His love for Christ goes way beyond the surface."

"What do you say, Amity?" Clem asked when they reached the end of the parking lot. "Don't you want to keep the part? You're very good at it and we'd hate to lose you before you even begin."

Amity bit her lip and gazed into the dark green of the woods, dappled with sunlight. It was true that she had good balance; she had never been clumsy and she was athletic. Maybe he was right that she had nothing to fear.

"I'll try it," she said, turning to go back. "Perhaps I can practice the run a few more times and see how it works. Dani may be able to coach me."

"I trust Dani has been helpful to you the past few nights?"

"Very. She went out of her way to make me feel welcome, and I've appreciated it."

"She thinks you're great." He shook his head. "You're just about all she's talked about since she met you last week."

"I wish you could say as much for my aunt."

His face creased in a brief smile. "Were you reading my mind?" He sighed. "There was a time when I thought some magic might happen between those two, but no more." He absently plucked a shaft of stray prairie grass. "I don't understand it."

"I'm sure Dani feels she has a good reason."

"Don't get the wrong idea about my daughter, Amity. She isn't the jealous or envious type. That's what confuses me. I thought she liked Enid at first. I suppose her mother. . ." he began, then stopped, as if realizing he had revealed more then he had intended to. "I won't let her chase Enid away."

"Don't forget that Enid has an independent nature," Amity warned him. "She'll make her own decisions."

Clem chuckled. "Don't I know it. But I can be stubborn and I usually find a way to get what I want. Especially if I decide that's what is best for my daughter and me."

"And you've decided Enid is?"

"Nothing could be better for either of us. I'd venture to guess that we would be good for her, too, if she would only give us a chance." He slowed his steps, his gaze fixed on someone near the dressing rooms.

Amity glanced up to see Nelson, leaning casually against a wall. He nodded to her.

"Looks like you've got another admirer," Clem remarked quietly.

"Another one?"

"Besides Titus," Clem said as Titus came down the steps and stood beside Nelson. The men waited for Clem and Amity to join them.

"Did she talk herself out of it?" Titus asked.

"No, I didn't," she said. "Not yet, anyway."

"If you're referring to the part," Clem told Titus, "I think she was afraid of falling. I assured her that there was little chance of that." He clapped Titus on the shoulder and walked up the stairs to the dressing room.

Nelson straightened from the wall. "You want to quit the play?"

"Yes. . .well. . ."

"She's getting the last-minute jitters," Titus said, watching her expression.

Amity stepped toward him and his bearded face blurred to her sight. She stumbled on the sidewalk. He rushed forward and caught her arm as the ground whirled beneath her feet.

Nelson caught her on the other side, and they led her to the steps to sit down.

"I'm sorry," she said shakily. "I knew I should have eaten tonight."

"Put your head down between your knees," Titus instructed, still holding her.

She obeyed and the darkness receded. She breathed deeply and sat up.

"I'm beginning to see why you don't want to run in the play," Titus said.

She moved to stand and both men helped her up.

"Maybe she shouldn't go on tonight," Nelson suggested. "What if this happens again?"

"I'm fine," she insisted, pulling from Nelson's grasp. "But you'd better get dressed. Don't let me hold you up."

"Are you sure?"

"Positive."

Nelson glanced at Titus, turned, and then left them with obvious reluctance.

"How are you feeling now?" Titus asked.

"I'm okay."

He lifted her chin firmly and she caught her breath. He ran a gentle thumb beneath her eyes, tracing the dark circles, caressing her cheek. Her heart beat more loudly against her ribs. His touch felt so good, so calming. . .and yet also disturbing.

"I don't think you're okay," he said.

"Of course I am." She refused to meet his eyes. "We both need to get our costumes on," she said quietly.

"Yes, I know," he said.

She heard the reluctance in his voice and she glanced up to find him still watching her quizzically. "Be careful," he said.

"I will," she answered.

Amity watched him climb swiftly up the steps and out of sight. With a quiet sigh, she walked toward her group room, his image filling her mind and blocking out all else. Lately, his powerful presence was too much for her to ignore. She had begun to search for his familiar form anytime he was not directly in her sight.

Clem met her at the wardrobe counter with her costume for the night. "You have a week before you're on, Mary Magdalene." He leaned forward and murmured, "Dani, of course, knows all the actions and lines for the part, and I know it would really please her if you asked for her help, as you'd mentioned doing."

"Of course. Where is Dani?"

"Right here," came a bright, cheerful voice directly behind Amity. Dani was already dressed, her hair shining with a golden dazzle against the soft pink of the material of her costume. "What are you two up to, with your heads together like that?" she teased, then she noticed Amity's state of dress. "Oh, Amity, you don't have your costume on yet! You'd better hurry!" She went with Amity to the ladies' dressing room and leaned against the wall as Amity changed into her costume.

"Amity," Dani said pensively, "do you think I'm too young to fall in love?"

Amity looked up in surprise, and tangled her hair in her headpiece. "You're never too young to love, Dani, but sometimes 'falling in love' isn't love at all, but just attraction. Who's the guy?"

Dani smiled. "Jason, the guy who plays the Apostle James. He's so good-looking."

"Don't mistake physical attraction for love," Amity warned. "That's such an easy thing to do. I should know. I've made that mistake."

Dani nodded. "I think that's what Dad did with Mother, and look at what a catastrophe that was!"

Amity looked at Dani thoughtfully. "No, he got you out of the deal, and I know he loves you very much." She gently tugged a strand of Dani's hair. "You may not be too young to love, but your father isn't too old, either, even as ancient as he is," she said dryly. "He isn't too old to love, or to be hurt by those he loves."

Without waiting for a reply, Amity entered the crowd of people and wove her way through to Darla, who was collecting her clothes at the counter. Darla barely had time to pull her costume on when the prelude music ended and the others started filing out.

"This promises to be a hectic night," the redhead predicted as the two of them climbed the steps to the Via Dolorosa. "Uh-oh, I should have known," she said, lowering her voice conspiratorially. "Here comes Nelson looking for you. He'll probably want me to get lost. Do you want to be alone with him?" She darted a teasing glance at Amity.

"Why should I? Besides, he's supposed to be with the crowd coming in with Jesus."

"Well, he's not, he's coming to talk to you, and I don't want to be in the way."

With growing impatience, Amity glanced around at him. "Oh, all right, let me talk to him, but not for long. He needs to back off. Guess I'll just have to get firm."

As Darla moved away to chatter with some other women on the street of Jerusalem, Nelson fell into step beside Amity. He slipped his hand beneath her elbow.

She drew away gently. "I don't think the directors would appreciate that. They probably didn't do this kind of thing in Jesus' time."

"What, touch?" Nelson snorted, but at her look, he released her. "Are you feeling better now? You had me worried."

"Yes, Nelson, I'm fine. Aren't you supposed to be with the Jesus group?"

"It's no big deal. No one pays any attention, anyway."

Amity could hardly conceal her annoyance as she looked up into his face. "You really feel that way?"

"Of course. No one counts how many people are with Jesus every night."

"But the directors want you there."

"They'll live through it, just this once," Nelson said. "Besides, I was worried about you. What caused you to faint? Titus said you just hadn't eaten, but I noticed he didn't go out of his way to get you something to eat. Why don't you let me take you out after the play and get you something hot? There's a good twenty-four-hour pancake place up in the new part of town." He eyed her critically. "You still don't look so great."

"Thanks." Amity's voice was dry. "But I think I'll survive. I'd better catch up with Darla now." She moved away but he caught her arm again.

"Amity, wait. I want to ask you something." He tugged at her arm until she stopped and faced him.

"What is it, Nelson?"

"You told me once that you and Titus were just good friends. Is that a euphemism for something else? You two are always together."

"What do you mean by 'euphemism'?" she asked sharply.

"Oh, come on," he snapped. "You're so eager to do everything he says, no questions asked, and you never let him out of your sight. It's almost as if you had some special relationship with him." His voice lowered and he said knowingly. "I know you live in the same house."

"I live with my aunt and he's a boarder there. End of story, not that it's any of your business."

"How convenient."

Amity wanted to slap him but she jerked away from him angrily. "Titus is a friend of mine, a good friend, but really, what is that to you? Nelson, I'm not in the market for a boyfriend right now, and if I were, I wouldn't want you telling me who it would be. Now, if you'll excuse me, I think Darla is waiting for me on the porch steps." She turned away and marched toward her friend.

As she searched the crowd for Darla, her gaze was drawn

to the group that surrounded Jesus. Titus was there and Amity felt a jolt of shock to find Titus's frowning attention on her.

When he came close enough to speak to her, he said, "I could have sworn Nelson was supposed to be with the apostles tonight. Looks like something more interesting caught his attention."

Before she could reply, the speaking parts began, and she found her way to Darla's side.

The crowd formed a semicircle around Jesus as he argued with the Sanhedrin on the temple steps, and Amity joined them, facing Titus. Every time she glanced toward him, he was watching her.

He caught up with her and Darla later as they walked up the via toward their dressing rooms. He fell into step with Amity.

"Have you been watching the movements of Mary Magdalene tonight?" Titus asked.

She started guiltily. "Not the way I should have." She had been upset by Nelson's attitude and insinuations.

"I thought you seemed a little preoccupied." He lowered his voice. "Are you still feeling ill?"

"No, I'm okay now, thanks. I'm sorry. I'll watch Mary for the rest of the play."

Darla, finished with her part, had not waited for the final scene, but had left for home as soon as she was dressed, and Amity had to walk down the via alone. Remembering Titus's orders to stay around other people, she hurried as quickly as she could toward the dressing rooms during the final scene.

"Amity!" Dani called from below as Amity stepped down toward her. "Did you see Jason tonight? What did you think? Isn't he cute?" Her eyes danced with excitement.

"I saw him. He was the one with the black beard and hair, wasn't he?"

"Yes, that was him! What did you think?"

"Cute," Amity agreed.

The inner dressing room was empty when they stepped inside to change. Dani cast Amity several surreptitious glances, cleared her throat several times, and finally sighed.

"I've been thinking about what you said earlier about Dad being hurt by the one he loves," Dani said. She sat down on the bench and tied her shoes.

Amity joined her. "What did you decide?"

"That I'm not always nice to everybody."

Amity finished buttoning her blouse. "In what way?"

"I don't want to hurt Dad. I want to try to be more open-minded about Enid. I'm not promising it'll work, just that I'll try."

Amity finished tying her shoes, straightened, and stood. "That's my—"

Dani's face swam out of focus and disappeared in darkness as Amity's legs gave way beneath her. She tried to grab the wall, but her arms refused to function. She fell hard against the concrete floor. Dani's piercing scream rose, then diminished, as if she were disappearing through a long tunnel.

Distant voices reached Amity's ears, but her eyes refused to open. She could almost hear what they were saying at times, but then the voices faded again. She struggled a few more moments, until the voices came closer and finally burst through her brain like a jet on a runway.

"Has she been out for long?" It was Titus speaking. "Dani, call the hospital and tell them I'm bringing her in."

Amity felt his strong arms move beneath her and lift her from the hard floor. She stirred, struggling to pry open eyelids that felt weighted with bags of sand. Gradually, she succeeded and a navy, cotton shirt came into immediate focus.

Her gaze traveled slowly up a muscled column of neck and dark beard to come to an abrupt halt at Titus's worried eyes. "No doctor," she managed to say with a tongue that felt wrapped in gauze. "No hospital. I'm fine; I just got up too fast. I've always fainted easily." Strength seeped slowly back into her body, and she could have sworn it came straight from Titus. His very touch revitalized her with every beat of his powerful heart.

He carried her into the main room and, at her insistence, sat her down on one of the benches. Dani, her eyes wide and anxious, rushed to sit down beside her. Amity patted the teenager's knee comfortingly. Other members of the cast gathered around her and she managed to assure them that she was okay. One by one, satisfied that it was nothing serious, they ambled away.

"That was once too often," Titus declared. "Time for you to see a doctor."

"Okay, okay, but not tonight." She flinched as he ran a hand across her forehead and tipped her chin up so he could see her eyes.

"Tomorrow, then," he said.

"We'll see," Amity responded.

"No, I'll make an appointment and I'll take you there myself. You're going. You don't have a fever, you aren't hungry, and this makes the second time today you've fainted. By tomorrow night I intend to know what's wrong with you."

ten

Monday morning the dawning sun came all too soon for Amity. Today was the day. No more denial. Any relationship she and Titus might have had was swept away by the possible secret hiding in her womb. She had just been fooling herself these past weeks, anyway.

To Amity's dismay, before she even got out of bed, that old familiar nausea began in the pit of her stomach, and she lay there a few more moments.

The birds sang merrily through her open window, flying from branch to branch of the old oak tree, and Amity scowled at them. What little sleep she had had last night had been filled with troubled dreams, dreams in which some faceless monster chased her through her home in Oklahoma City, threatening to kill her. There was one dream that had been worse. In it she had seen Titus turn from her with revulsion when he discovered she was pregnant.

She knew Titus was saving himself for his future wife. In this world of casual sex, even among people who called themselves Christians, a man who kept himself pure was a precious treasure, deserving of a woman who was just as pure and worthy. Amity felt she was neither. She felt as if she were carrying excess baggage with her. How could she ever expect any man to want her the way she was?

She closed her eyes, but once again visions stirred of the faceless stranger who wanted her dead and who threatened to kill her if she did not produce something she did not have. What had Chad confessed to? And how could she have married a man who had had so little regard for human decency?

She stared out the window and placed a protective hand

across her abdomen. If she were carrying a baby, whatever happened to her would happen to her baby. She might have twice the reason to be terrified of those faceless bogeymen.

"Oh, dear Lord, please protect me," she whispered. "And give me faith. Somewhere along the way I've become too frightened to trust You. Please forgive me, and help me." She paused. "And, Lord, please take care of my baby. . .if. . ."

The rumbling in her stomach, far from settling, threatened to boil over at any moment, and she climbed from bed, steadying herself against the wall. She dragged her robe from the bedside chair and managed to wrap it around her shoulders. She felt as weak as a drowning duck and it was an effort to tie the sash with her fingers shaking so much.

But she had to hurry if she was going to make it to the bathroom in time, so she forced herself forward, rushed out of the room, down the stairs, and to the third-floor bathroom. It was locked. The sound of running water barely reached her ears before she was rushing down the second floor, steadying herself against the walls. She was getting dizzier, sicker, and she prayed she would make it and not have an embarrassing accident out in the hallway.

The second-floor bathroom was empty, but the wave of relief she felt lasted only an instant before the nausea struck again. She stumbled into the bathroom and pushed the door closed behind her.

She was just in time. Her legs trembled weakly as she stood above the basin, losing what little bit Titus had forced her to eat before she went to bed. Perspiration covered her body, soaking her nightgown and dampening her hair.

Someone knocked on the door. "Amity?" It was Titus. "Amity, are you in there?"

"Go away."

"Are you sick?"

"Just go away," she said miserably.

"Open the door, Amity."

"Can't I have any privacy?"

There was a long hesitation. "Sorry. I just wanted to make sure you were okay."

He was still waiting when she stepped out the door a few moments later. He kept a guiding hand on her arm and walked close beside her as she went back up the stairs and into her bedroom. Still weak and shaky, she lay down on top of the rumpled covers of her bed.

"Thank you," she whispered.

Despite her misery and embarrassment, one small part of her mind registered the fact that his large frame overpowered her tiny bedroom. Or perhaps it was his overwhelming presence.

He sat down beside her and straightened her hair, combing through it with his fingers. "Better now?"

She nodded, unable to drag her gaze from the tender expression in his eyes.

"Does Enid know you're pregnant?" he asked gently.

She closed her eyes and shook her head. Tears formed beneath her lids—she could feel the stinging heat of them— and no matter how tightly she closed her eyes, the hot droplets still pushed their way out to spill down her cheeks.

The first sob rose in her throat, and she felt Titus's comforting arms lifting her up to bury her face against the soft material of his shirt. She could not stop the tears once they started.

Titus appeared oblivious to the soaking his shoulder was receiving, so intent was he on rocking her in his arms and crooning soft words of comfort in her ear.

"It's going to be okay, Amity," he whispered, smoothing her hair. "You're not alone. Don't worry." His voice sounded indulgent, even loving.

Her sobs gradually eased, and she braved a glance at him.

His expression held only warmth and tenderness. . .and a hint of some other emotion she dared not try to analyze.

She reached across to tug a tissue from its box on the

bedside table and dried her face. Then she blew her nose. This was ridiculous.

"I'm sorry I'm being such a baby about all this," she said. "I'm not usually so weepy."

"Don't you think I know that by now? You've had too much burden on your shoulders lately," he said, taking the tissue from her and tossing it into the wastebasket beside the table. He pulled out another one and handed it to her. "I'd say you were handling this well. Most others would have fallen apart by now."

"I am, piece by piece. Some Christian, huh?"

"Stop that. How long have you known you were pregnant?"

"I don't even know for sure that I am, since I haven't been to the doctor."

"Never been to the doctor at all! But surely you've known about—"

"I've suspected it for a while. There was just so much to think about, so much to do, that I pushed it to the back of my mind, hoping it wasn't true."

Titus leaned forward. "Why would you hope that? A baby is a wonderful thing, a renewal of life."

"And a tremendous responsibility I'm not sure I can handle. Not like this. Not without a father, while I'm running from some unknown killer!"

"Avoiding the truth will not help anything. I'm going to go talk to Enid while you get dressed, then we'll go to the doctor. Everything will be okay from now on." He bent over, kissed her cheek, and turned to leave.

She watched bemusedly as he walked out of her room and down the attic steps. Then she got ready to take a shower.

The pleasant heat of the shower felt heavenly against her skin, and she hummed to herself as she scrubbed, feeling more confident with each passing moment. Titus was taking care of everything. Her burden, though still lurking back there, somewhere in the recesses of her mind, had lifted enough to give her a glimpse of sunshine where before had been only darkness.

"Thank You, Lord," she murmured as she stepped out of the shower. "What a wonderful answer to my prayer." Titus's kindness and gentleness had seemed to reflect God's own tender love.

She returned to her room refreshed in body and spirit, and she inhaled with pleasure the soft, drifting scent of honeysuckle that grew on a trellis just below her window. Light footfalls coming up from the attic steps alerted Amity to Enid's presence just before her aunt knocked.

"Come in," Amity called. She took a deep, sustaining breath, and turned toward the door.

Enid's eyes, as she stepped into the bedroom, were troubled. "Titus said you were feeling ill. What are you doing up?"

"Getting ready to go to the doctor. Titus insisted." So Titus had not told Enid about the pregnancy.

"Well, it's about time he talked some sense into you." Enid touched Amity's forehead. "No fever." Her hazel eyes narrowed and she surveyed Amity's face. "Titus said you were sick a while ago." She sat down on the edge of Amity's bed, still watching Amity expectantly, as if waiting for an answer to an unvoiced question.

"I was. I'm better now." Amity peeled off her robe and selected a pair of slacks to wear. It was so easy to fall into the old habit of ignoring the problem. It seemed so easy to forget it all, and so hard to talk about after all these weeks.

"Titus didn't say what kind of doctor he was taking you to," Enid prompted.

Amity picked up a clinging, red knit top, pulled it over her head, glanced in the mirror, and pulled it off again. "No, he didn't tell me, either. He seemed to know what he was doing, so I just left it up to him." She chose a loose, white cotton top and put it on.

Enid expelled a sigh of exasperation and stood to her feet,

her slender, tanned arms folded across her chest. "Well?"

Amity bit her lip.

"Amity, I've given you plenty of time to offer the information. Is it possible you're pregnant?"

"Yes," Amity replied. Her chin began to tremble. This was so frustrating, this constant fluctuation of her emotions. "Yes, Aunt Enid, it's very possible. I would say even probable, at this point." She stepped into a pair of baggy trousers.

"Well, don't cry about it!" Enid caught her niece in a bear hug. "A baby! My grandniece! Your own, very own baby!"

"Don't get carried away. I'm not sure about it yet. And remember that if I am pregnant, the baby won't have a father." Amity shook her head. "It's funny, isn't it, Aunt Enid? I was always the one among my friends in college who had sworn to remain a virgin until I married. For me, it was the only way. I saw a lot of girls get pregnant and drop out of school. Some even had abortions." She shuddered, thinking of Dani's mother. "I insisted nothing like that would ever happen to me." She slumped on the edge of the bed. "Never say never."

"Honey, that isn't what happened to you." Enid sat down beside her and put an arm around her shoulders. "If you're pregnant, the baby will be perfectly legitimate."

"But I'll still be a single mother, with all the trials and hardships to go with it."

Enid shook her head sharply. "No, you won't. I want you to stay here with me."

Amity stood and paced to the dresser. She picked up a brush, idly pulled it through her hair, then set it down again. "What about Clem?" She glanced at her aunt's reflection in the mirror. "You can't drag me along when you marry him."

Enid raised a silencing hand. "No. We won't even discuss that. He is out of the picture."

"That's not true and you know it. Be realistic. I've seen how you two feel about each other. I also know about your problems. But just last night, Dani promised me she would stop blaming you for problems she's had in the past. She wants to try harder to accept you."

Enid looked surprised for a moment. "Well," she said consideringly, then shook her head. "Nevertheless, we aren't discussing my problems right now, we're discussing yours, and you'll be welcome in any home of mine or it won't remain my home."

Amity could not suppress a grin. "I know, I know. But you'll have to fight Mom and Dad to keep them from dragging me back to Oklahoma City when they find out." She sighed and shook her head. "I know I'm always welcome with family. But I can't do that forever. I'm a grown woman and I need to shoulder my own responsibilities."

Enid frowned. "You always were an independent little monster. It isn't as if you don't have money, though. One thing Chad did do was leave you well-provided for."

"Okay, but how could I drag a baby into the middle of this mess I'm in, not knowing if Chad's killer is lurking around the next corner?"

"If you're pregnant you have no choice, honey, so stop fighting it and do the best you can. You have my full support, you know." Enid stepped up behind Amity at the mirror, watching her. "Have faith in God. I know I struggle during the hard times, but He has shown me His faithfulness in every situation in my life."

Amity smiled. "Same here. I wish I were more trusting. I have to keep reminding myself that God is in control in all circumstances, and if there is a baby, God will be faithful there, too. It's my own human weakness that makes me panic at what might be in store for the future."

"If it were anyone else, I would suggest adoption."

Amity stared at her aunt, shocked. "Aunt Enid!"

"I meant to me and. . .well, that is. . .if Clem and I do happen to get together." She grimaced wryly. "No, I guess not. It's just that I always did want a little one."

"I know you always did." She raised a brow at her aunt. "You know, it isn't too late to have a baby yourself."

Enid chuckled. "I don't know why we're even having this conversation, kiddo. God will take care of everything." Her eyes twinkled. "And I think I can see just how He's planning to do it."

"How?"

"Titus King, that's how."

"Titus? What does he have to do with it?"

"Don't play games with me, Amity Hudson. The two of you are perfect together. Look who's taking you to the doctor. It should be me but no, Titus took over."

"That's only because you're so busy."

"With Opal helping? Nonsense. If I were a betting woman, I'd be willing to wager that he already knows you're pregnant." She quirked a brow at Amity. "I'm right, aren't I?"

"Aunt Enid, it was—"

"No," Enid said with an uplifted hand, "don't try to explain it away. I know an old-maid aunt can't take the place of a strong, warm-blooded man in your life."

"Aunt Enid! What a ridiculous idea! You're about as much of an old maid as I am Santa Claus. We aren't even sure, yet, that I'm pregnant, and furthermore, Titus guessed about my pregnancy, just like you did. Besides, I wouldn't marry a man just to tie him down with someone else's baby."

Enid grinned. "Titus loves children."

"So? That's nothing to base a marriage on, and I haven't known Titus long enough. I'm not about to make the same mistake I made with Chad."

"Titus is nothing like Chad. I never did approve of Chad, and I do Titus. He's a solid, mature Christian man who is more than ready to settle down with the right woman. If you were honest with yourself, you'd have to admit that."

"But what if I'm not the right woman for him? He deserves—"

"Someone who will love him and serve God with him. I think you are that person. You've known each other since last fall and this spring you've been in such close proximity you couldn't help but get to know each other better than most people who've been dating several months."

"He doesn't need a ready-made family."

"If the child belongs to the right woman—"

Further argument was silenced by a firm rap on the door.

"Are you ready?" Titus asked.

"Well, I should be getting back to my cooking." Enid pulled open the door and let Titus in. "Take good care of her. She's the only niece I have."

When they were alone, Amity avoided his gaze. She brushed her hair and checked around the room once more, but after stalling as long as she could, she turned to face Titus.

She raised reluctant green eyes to his, and what she saw there sent tingles of anticipation up her spine. He exuded such strength, yet it was tempered with such tenderness just now. His eyes softened as they held hers and, in spite of herself, her heart answered him with all the longing inside her.

Then she remembered her own words to her aunt, about tying a man down with someone else's baby. Taking a deep breath and steeling herself against his magnetism, she tore her gaze from his. This was going to be harder than she expected. Titus King was a hard man to ignore, as she had known for some time.

"Are you ready?" he asked.

She nodded, and preceded him out the door.

"Now I understand," Titus said as he propelled the Jeep around the curve of the mountain.

"Understand?"

"About the Mary Magdalene part. You didn't want to take any chances on hurting the baby." He glanced at her briefly before turning up a steep, narrow lane, bordered on both sides by well-kept trees and shrubs. "I'm sorry I insisted you take the part."

"How could you have known? We still don't know for sure."

"But if you are?" he asked as he pulled the Jeep to a stop on a white gravel driveway in front of a long, red brick house.

"I want to wait until I know for sure before I make any more plans."

She stepped out of the Jeep. At the north end of the house was a door bearing a large sign: Dr. J. O'Toole, M.D.

Titus took Amity's arm and guided her along a white, curving sidewalk that stretched between sections of green, well-manicured lawn.

Amity's throat constricted as Titus opened the door. The usual waiting room scents of old magazines and antiseptic wafted out to greet her. She hesitated a moment, swallowing hard.

Titus touched her arm. "Amity?"

She nodded and stepped inside.

&

Examination finished, Amity was prepared to walk back into the waiting room when a nurse spoke behind her.

"Are you ready to talk with the doctor now, Amity?"

Amity jerked around. "Y–yes, I guess I am."

"Right this way." The nurse turned and walked a few steps down the short hallway. "He's in here," she said, stopping to open a door. "We thought your husband would like to sit in on this one." She grinned and winked, then ushered a frowning, hesitant Amity in and closed the door behind her.

Despite the nurse's announcement, the sight of Titus, sitting with nonchalant ease across the desk from the doctor shocked Amity.

"What are you doing here?" she asked.

Doctor O'Toole peered at her over the rim of his glasses. "It's our practice to counsel both the mother and father together. I assume you do both want the baby?"

Amity slumped weakly into a chair beside Titus. So she really was pregnant. "Y–yes. That is, I want the baby, but—"

"Yes, Doctor," Titus interrupted smoothly, slanting an amused glance at Amity. "We both want this baby. You're saying the test was positive?"

The doctor nodded, beaming at them both. "Congratulations. According to my calculations, your baby is due in about six and a half months." He leaned back in his chair and regarded them both with a benevolent smile. "I trust you plan to have prenatal care?"

"Of course," Titus replied.

"Good." The doctor went on to explain their usual prenatal procedure.

Amity listened with only half her attention as she struggled with confusion and the realization that she was actually going to have a baby. There was no turning back, no more ignoring symptoms. In less than seven months, God willing, she would be holding her own tiny baby in her arms. Her whole body trembled with the utter terror, and the sweet ecstasy of it.

The remainder of the visit passed in a fog. It was only when she and Titus emerged—a seeming eternity later—from the air-conditioned office, that she began to feel the reality of it.

The world came alive around her as she walked beside Titus toward the Jeep. The sidewalk and driveway were glaringly white, and the irises in the doctor's garden smelled wonderful as the sun beat down on their delicate petals. The sky was so blue it hurt her eyes and her head felt light, as if it floated several inches above her body. Had the doctor slipped her a drug of some kind while she was in there? She felt like not only her head, but her whole body was floating. And she could not keep from smiling. What was wrong with her?

"It's a beautiful day," she said with a sigh as she climbed into her seat. She met Titus's smiling gaze. "I shouldn't feel that way, should I?"

"You most certainly should." He walked around the front

of the vehicle. "Life is something to celebrate."

They drove around the circular driveway and back down the secluded lane, and Amity's senses continued to feel more sharply, see more clearly, smell and hear more perfectly. She felt fully alive, vigorous, strong.

"If you're feeling up to it," Titus suggested, "I'll take you on that New Holy Land tour I promised you."

"I never felt better." She glanced at him. "Why did you tell them you were my husband?"

"I told them nothing of the sort." He chuckled. "They just took for granted that I was."

She shook her head. "They could just as easily have taken you to be my brother, since our eyes are the same color."

"They didn't. They thought I was your husband. . .the baby's father."

"Well, why didn't you tell them otherwise? It's going to be embarrassing when I have to go back and explain everything."

"I detest lying."

"Lying?"

Titus stopped the Jeep at the bottom of the hill and turned slowly to face Amity. "I have every intention of becoming your baby's father," he stated confidently.

eleven

"No." Amity barely heard the sound of her own voice over the pounding of her heart. If only things had been different. . .

"Why not?" Titus asked.

She looked across at him. "I would never take advantage of you like that. It would be wrong."

Titus put the Jeep into gear and turned onto the highway. "That's not what this is."

"How can you say that? You're offering to marry me so my baby can have a father. That's almost as bad as the reason I married Chad."

"I believe it would have come to this, anyway." He glanced at her. "At least, I'd hoped."

Amity leaned back in her seat and watched the scenery. "I don't have any idea what would have happened, Titus. Maybe. . .I just can't think about that now."

He pulled to the side of the road and parked beneath a pair of towering oak trees. A tiny spring of sparkling water trickled down the mossy cracks of a rock, and Amity stared at it rather than face him. He reached out to turn her to him and she jumped when she felt the warm strength of his hands on her shoulders. She kept her eyes lowered.

"Amity, your baby needs a father. The natural father will never be able to take that responsibility." He grasped her chin with thumb and forefinger, forcing her to meet his gaze. "I want that responsibility, Amity. I'm ready for it."

A breeze gently stirred tendrils of hair around her face as his words echoed through her mind. The splashing of the spring grew louder.

"I know a baby needs a family," she said. "But not a family

that will break up because the husband and wife married for the wrong reasons in the first place."

Titus took her by the shoulders. "Tell me you wouldn't have married me if you weren't carrying a baby."

She looked away.

"No, you can't say it, can you?"

"If I weren't pregnant, you wouldn't have asked me, Titus. Not now. Not yet. You would have waited—"

"And we will wait. It's not like I'm asking you to marry me tomorrow." He released her and lifted a strand of her hair, running its silky softness through his fingers. "I knew, almost from our first meeting, that you were someone special. That knowledge grew stronger the more I came to know you."

"I don't believe in love at first sight," she said. "Especially not after being married to Chad."

"I'm not talking about love at first sight. I don't believe in that, either. But we've come to know each other well, Amity. In many respects, we've come to know each other much more quickly than most people because we are staying in the same house."

"Titus, I'm not saying I don't believe in love, just not love at first sight. Knowing each other isn't good enough. You've never even told me you loved me."

He stared at her for a moment. "Isn't that what this is all about? Love in its deepest sense?"

"Are you saying you're in love with me?"

He frowned. "Amity, I've never been in love before. I've always regarded it as some deep, mysterious event that happens and you can't control it but that it controls you."

"So you don't love me." The pain she felt at his words told her, more than anything, how deeply she felt about him. But as she had said, mere feelings were not enough. Amazing how powerfully they could control a person, though.

"I love spending time with you," he said. "I miss you constantly when we're not together, and I don't think I can stand the thought of not having you in my life. As time passes, I want to be with you more and more. I like you, too, Amity. You're my best friend on this earth, and this is not some light-hearted infatuation. You tell me, since you seem to know, is this what you call being in love? I'm not experienced with this kind of thing. I just don't know."

"When it's love, you'll know."

"Did you know with Chad?"

"I obviously didn't love Chad," she said bitterly. "Maybe I've never known love, either. Maybe I'm not even capable of love."

"Don't be so hard on yourself. Look at the way your husband treated you."

"Last year I treated you very shabbily, too," she said. "Every time I think about it—"

"Don't think about it. I don't think I understood what was happening to me until I received your letter about Chad. I know now, and it's more than just a 'feeling.' There's more between us than physical attraction." Without waiting for a reply, he started the motor and pulled onto the road again. "If not, I'll give you plenty of time to discover that for yourself, but I'm not giving up."

They soon reached the big, white gate that led to the New Holy Land and this time, instead of parking, Titus drove through the entrance, past the animal pens, and down a rocky dirt road.

Titus became the perfect guide. His deep, compelling voice soothed Amity, and she let it wash over her as she soaked up tidbits of interesting information. She had never known anyone who could put her so at ease and whose company she enjoyed so much, even in times of peaceful silence.

As he talked, they traveled the rough road down a steep mountainside into the valley below. The fragrance of freshly mown hay wafted across to them from some unseen hay field. No domesticated, tended flowers grew here, but the hillsides were covered with a vast variety of wildflowers. Red, purple, yellow, and white greeted her with their brightness, and she barely resisted asking Titus to stop so she could pick a handful of the daisies.

"Have you heard of the legend of the dogwood?" Titus asked, slowing to a stop beside two trees covered with white blooms.

"Isn't that supposed to be the type of tree that was used for the crucifixion of Christ?"

"Yes, that's one legend. According to that, the dogwood was once as strong and mighty as one of those oaks." He pointed to a tree across the road, its trunk half as big around as the Jeep. "When the tree was forced into service as the cross of Jesus Christ, it was so heartbroken that God promised it would never again grow big enough to be used for such a crime. Its petals, two short and two long, are said to represent the cross, while the rusty stain in the middle of each represent the nails and the blood. There is also a circle within the bloom that represents the crown of thorns."

"The legend could be true, couldn't it?" Amity said. "How like God to make something beautiful out of heartbreak."

"Right, Amity," Titus said quietly. "He always sends us help for our trials. I just wish you could accept the fact that God sent me to be your help."

She bit her lip thoughtfully, without replying, and he drove on, crossing a tiny stream that trickled over the road. Titus turned at a fork in the road and followed a stream to the right. Ahead of them, Amity saw a huge rock structure, like a cave with a huge slab of stone laid across the top to form a roof.

"This," Titus informed her, as he parked and climbed out, "is a cave representing the birthplace of Jesus." He came around to Amity's door, opened it for her, and waited for her to get out.

She stared at him, then at the cave, puzzled. What did this have to do with the Holy Land?

"Didn't you realize Jesus was born in a cave of rock?" he asked.

"I thought it was a stable."

"This is a stable, see? There are statues of animals in there along with the people. Trees were so scarce in Bethlehem at the time of Jesus' birth that when people could, they built their stables and their homes in caves, or with rock. Jesus' cradle was hewn out of rock. People certainly wouldn't have wasted their precious wood on an old stable manger."

Amity nodded. "They couldn't have known their Savior would be born there. How did you build this rock to look so natural?"

Titus took her hand and strolled with her up to the edge of the cave. "It was already here. Except for that slab of rock on top, this used to be someone's cellar. It turned out to be a perfect place for this display. We've had several such coincidences since the statue was built, but we call them miracles."

He parked the Jeep at a dam and they got out. The sun shone brightly on a miniature lake and a breeze stirred the water until it rippled into a million tiny reflections of the sky. Titus led Amity across a footbridge that spanned the dam.

"See what I mean? As small as this is, this Sea of Galilee is situated just in the right place to catch the wind as it whistles down through that gully." He pointed to an opening in the mountains directly across the lake.

"Here's my favorite spot," he said, leading her to a small stone bench, placed in the shade of an overhanging elm tree.

She allowed herself to be drawn down to sit beside him. "It's cool and peaceful here."

"Yes, it is, isn't it?"

"You've done a wonderful job, Titus."

"I'm just one advisor among many." He leaned back, stretching his long legs in front of him. "They've put a lot of years of study and labor into this, and we have a long way to go before it's finished. You can see some of the buildings through the trees along that ridge," he said, pointing across the lake. "All you can see are the outlines, but they're reproductions of some major buildings in old Jerusalem. The land I have in mind for our school is connected to this land."

"Your school," Amity said.

"As my wife, I hope you will have a lot of interest in the school." Titus trailed a finger down her arm to her hand, then clasped it tightly in his own.

"Titus, you're taking for granted that I'm going to marry you, but—"

"Haven't you discovered anything on this tour?" he asked. "The first place I took you. . .Jesus' birthplace. . .didn't that stir your memory?"

"For what?"

"Joseph was a stepfather. God, in all His wisdom, provided an earthly father for His Son. What better way can I convince you?"

Amity stared at his fingers, now intertwined with her own. They just fit. Slowly, he brought her hand up to his mouth and pressed his lips against her skin. She closed her eyes, struggling to ward away the emotions that threatened to engulf her at his touch.

Why was she resisting him? Because of Chad? But hadn't Titus proved his Christianity, revealed his inner soul the way Chad had never done? She realized she was still fighting Chad, not Titus. The two men were worlds apart, both literally and figuratively. Wasn't it time for her to leave the nightmare of Chad behind?

A shadow fell across her closed eyes. She opened them, and found them reflected back at her in his, only his were filled with determination, whereas hers were only beginning to understand God's plan.

He pulled her forward until she rested her head on his broad shoulder. She felt his lips touch lightly in her hair.

"I understand, Amity, believe me," he said, his arms

tightening around her. "In your heart, you have wounds that you haven't allowed to heal, but you must let them. You asked me earlier if I'm in love with you. I love you with a love that only Christ could place in my heart. I think that's the best love of all. I cherish you, and I want to be with you always. Does that answer your question?"

"Yes." She smiled.

"But do you love me?"

Amity hesitated. "How can I trust my own feelings? I did before. . ."

"Don't you believe that our being together is God's will? Why else would circumstances have happened this way?"

"I can't say. I'm confused."

"Sweetheart, don't you believe in miracles? Not even here, where miracles are so prevalent?"

"I want to. . ." she sighed.

"What about the healing powers? Don't you remember the story I told you about the Indians and their healing springs? Amity, look at me."

She slowly tilted her head until she could look into his eyes.

"That promise of healing is within you. Jesus died for you in the healing passion. Don't turn away from something you already have within yourself."

She dropped her gaze. "What you're saying makes sense, but. . ."

"But what? It's simple. Just accept it. I'm not Chad, I'm nothing like him. I'm real, not a dream. Chad was a dream that went sour when you were faced with reality. He knew how to say all the right words, pull all the right strings, talk the right talk. We're two completely different men. Chad charmed you with a facade." He spread his hands in a self-deprecating gesture. "Look at me. I don't even know how to act around women. I've always been so absorbed in study and work, I haven't exactly developed social skills." He tilted her chin up until their eyes met. "But I can guarantee that as long as I've waited for the right woman to come into my life, I'm not about to abandon her emotionally, or take her for granted. You are the right woman. I will cherish my wife with everything I am."

"Yes, I know."

"Then what's stopping you from accepting me? Do you remember what you said the other day, about God leading you here for some reason? Don't you still believe that?"

"Yes," Amity said.

And at those words, everything fit. God had led her here to continue her life. He had led her to Titus, to Eureka Springs, to the school.

"Yes, I do." She sat up and turned to him, her gaze caressing his face. "You are God's gift of love to me, aren't you? Like He did with the dogwood, He's promising me beauty out of my pain."

The confusion melted away. Tears of happiness and relief filled her eyes. They spilled over to run down her cheeks, unheeded, as she buried her face against his shoulder. He hugged her to him and she wrapped her arms around him, squeezing him so tightly she was sure she would force the breath from him.

"Better now?" he asked a few moments later, when her tears of joy had dried and she rested peacefully in his arms.

She nodded. "This particular scene is becoming a habit."

"The tears?" Titus asked gently. "Then we'll have to see that it doesn't happen again." He lifted her chin and gazed tenderly into her tear-streaked face. "Amity, does this mean you'll marry me?"

"Yes," she whispered, "yes, I'll marry you. Oh, Titus, I do love you."

"Words straight from heaven," he murmured as he lowered his mouth to hers.

twelve

The road out of the New Holy Land seemed rougher, steeper than it had coming in, and Amity knew her face was pale by the time they reached the top. Her stomach began to roll in that familiar way.

Titus glanced at her and immediately stopped the vehicle. "Why didn't you say you were feeling ill?" He reached into the back seat of the Jeep for a roll of paper towels. After tearing a section off, he jumped from the Jeep and crossed the road to a tiny rivulet of water seeping out from a crack in the rocks.

He wet the towels and carried them back to place them on Amity's forehead. The icy water refreshed her immediately, quelling the threat of nausea.

"Thank you." She closed her eyes and relished the peace and happiness of the moment. "Right now, I feel I could be in heaven. How much better can it be?"

"For one thing," he said dryly, "I don't think there's morning sickness in heaven."

Soon they passed back beneath the Golden Gate, and Amity grimaced as she gazed out across the amphitheater. "There go my dreams of stardom. Dr. O'Toole certainly was adamant that I quit the part of Mary Magdalene."

"If he hadn't insisted, I would have," Titus said. "You could take almost any other part but that one. It's too risky."

Amity nodded, instinctively placing a protective hand over her abdomen. "Don't worry, I had already made up my mind not to take it, especially after I nearly tripped and fell last night in the dark." Her lips turned up in a wistful smile. "I remember how badly I wanted a baby when Chad and I were first married," she said. "I soon changed my mind when he started treating me so badly. I didn't want to take the chance that he would treat our child that way." She looked at Titus consideringly. "You'll make a wonderful father."

He looked at her and the wealth of love she saw made her catch her breath. He would make a good father, but he would also make a wonderful husband. Oh, how she loved him.

Enid was ecstatic when Amity and Titus returned home with the news, and even Opal, who had just finished the laundry for the day, postponed a sightseeing trip to celebrate with a festive lunch.

"What did I tell you?" Enid said, her hazel eyes glowing at the news that Titus and Amity were going to get married. "It's all worked out just as God had planned."

She set the table with her best china and would not let Amity or Titus make a move to help.

"I'll help with this lunch," Opal said, apparently as excited about the news as the rest of them. "I never saw a couple more suited for each other," she said, beaming at the two of them. "When is the wedding?"

Amity and Titus glanced at each other, and Amity shrugged. "We just decided to get married. We haven't decided when, or how, or anything about it."

Enid clapped her hands excitedly. "This is wonderful! I have a wedding to plan! I'll call your mother immediately after lunch, and we'll discuss it."

Amity held a hand up. "Wait! Don't you think I should break the news to her first? She's liable to panic if we hit her with everything at once."

Titus took Amity's hand and kissed her fingertips. "May I make one suggestion? I would like to get married at our church, where we hope to have our school someday. It will be a beautiful memory I want to cherish the rest of my life."

Amity's throat tightened with emotion and to cover up she stood up with the announcement that she would call her parents right away, and after that, she would call Farris, who, after all, would be the baby's aunt. She dashed out of the kitchen to the phone in the sitting room.

≈

"Well?" Enid asked later. "How did it go?"

Amity sat down to join them for a delicious lunch of baked chicken and dressing. "As I expected," she said with a rueful smile. "They're ecstatic. You know how much they adored Titus when we came down last year."

Opal joined them at the table as Enid took hot rolls out of the oven.

"I'll call them back this afternoon," Enid said after the blessing. "I can't wait to start the arrangements."

"Hold it, Aunt Enid," Amity warned. "This is not a shotgun wedding. It's not as if we're getting married tomorrow or next week. We're going to take our time and do it right."

"Honey, do you know how long it takes to plan a wedding right? Trust me, I'm not rushing you."

"I have a request," Titus said. "Amity, you've never met my parents. They know about you because I've talked to them about you, but I would like you to meet them soon."

"Absolutely," Enid agreed. "It's part of the engagement process. . .although the first meeting usually takes place before the engagement."

"Thank you, Emily Post," Amity said. "I want to meet them as soon as possible, but they're all the way down in Texas, and—"

"We'll fly."

"Okay. We'll set it up. Do you think we could stop by Oklahoma City on the way? I know my parents would love to see you again."

"Sounds good."

"Did you talk to Farris?" Enid asked. "Is she recovering from her accident?"

Amity sipped her water, a frown marring her forehead. "She seems okay, but she still doesn't remember anything about yesterday. She sounds—" Amity shot a glance at Opal, wondering how much to mention in front of the woman, "she sounds suspicious of me again, as if I had something to do with it."

They did not discuss more in front of Opal, and for the remainder of the day they made tentative plans for the wedding, plans for selling Amity's house in Oklahoma City, and plans for their school.

ða

During their quick trip to meet future in-laws, Amity visited Farris briefly, but although Farris softened when Amity talked about the baby, she still seemed edgy, suspicious, and unwilling to divulge any new information. It was an exhausting two days, and Amity was glad to get back to Eureka Springs, which she now considered to be her home.

Opal, seemingly a free agent, decided to stay at the lodge for a few more weeks, due to Amity's pregnancy and the coming wedding, and Enid was grateful. Business was now at its best, with all the rooms filled every night, and Enid was too involved with Clem and the wedding to concentrate fully on the lodge.

Titus, nearly always beside Amity with his reassurance and protective love, helped to alleviate her fears about Farris's accident. Nevertheless, Amity never ventured out alone and she always stayed with the cast members at the set.

To everyone's delight, Dani was chosen to take Amity's place as Mary Magdalene. Amity, still eager to participate in the play, readily accepted Dani's part as Salome.

Once more, Dani's sweet spirit became evident as she spent many hours coaching Amity on her part. By the night they were to take their new places, both had memorized their moves perfectly.

"Amity, wait up!" Dani called from below the stairs.

Amity glanced down to see the young girl, dressed in Mary Magdalene's costume, rushing up the stairs, two at a time, to catch her.

"Just think," Dani puffed, out of breath from practicing her part, "tonight's the night." She cocked her head sideways and, from beneath long, mascared lashes, peered up at Amity. "Are you scared?"

"Not at all," Amity assured the girl, draping an arm across Dani's shoulders. "Why should I be? You taught me well. By the way, happy birthday, sweet sixteen and—dare I say? —never been kissed."

Dani grinned and wrinkled her nose at Amity. "You can say anything you like, of course, but. . ." She shrugged expressively.

"What?" Amity exclaimed in mock horror. "Don't tell me Jason. . . ?"

"Well," Dani mumbled, blushing, "maybe just a little peck on the cheek. But still, that's a kiss, isn't it?"

"Absolutely. Want to practice our parts one more time before the play?"

Dani giggled. "As early as we are, we could practice both our parts several more times. Why is it that when we're doing a new part for the first time, we always get here at least an hour early?"

"I don't know about you, but since this is Friday night, I expect a full audience and I don't want to mess up too badly." Amity led the way toward the stage area. "I like to have time to get the feel of it."

"Not me," Dani said. "I just wanted to see Jason before the play." She glanced at Amity and giggled again at her friend's look of exasperation.

The rehearsal went smoothly and the two of them walked back into the dressing room, out of breath, to find the phone ringing.

"I'll get it," Dani said as she dashed toward the counter. "Hello? Yes, just a second." She held the receiver out for Amity, frowning. "It's for you. . .emergency."

Amity took the phone, her heart pounding more rapidly.

"Hello?"

"Amity? Oh, good." It was Farris.

Amity's fingers tightened convulsively around the receiver. "Yes. Farris, what's wrong?"

"Amity, I was wrong, I'm sorry. I know now that you didn't have anything to do with Chad's death, but whoever did it might be in Eureka Springs now and you've got to be careful!"

Amity gasped. "How do you know? What's happened?"

"My accident was no accident. I remember it now. Someone ran me off the road and I know it wasn't you."

The room whirled around Amity and she grasped the counter for support. "It's what I was afraid of," she croaked. "But how do you know it wasn't me?"

"Believe me, I know. I wasn't the only one who came to check on you." A heavy sigh came through the phone. "Oh, well, I suppose I can tell you some of it, since Uncle Jim just went to the police with Chad's confession. Chad's friends were blackmailing Uncle Jim. That was one of the reasons Chad wanted out. They. . .they discovered something about my uncle that he didn't want the public to know, since he's running for the senate. At first I had thought you might be in on it, and I had someone keeping an eye on you there while I was in Fayetteville. Amity, you've got to be careful! If those people are still there, there's no telling what they'll do to you!" She groaned with helpless frustration. "Look, whatever you do, stay close to Titus. He'd frighten anything away."

Amity swallowed to loosen the knot of terror that had begun to form in her chest. She glanced over at Dani, who watched her anxiously, her blue eyes darkening with worry.

"If you can't stay around Titus," Farris continued, "just stay close to anyone you can trust. Stay around people. These guys won't try anything then. Surely they won't. . ."

Amity glanced at Dani, hesitated, then blurted, "But what about the police? If Uncle Jim gave them Chad's confession, won't they arrest these people?"

"Sure, when they find them," Farris snapped. "In the meantime, don't take any chances. They don't know the police have the confession, so they'll still be after you. Just don't let them get you alone! Stay around people."

"That's what I've been doing ever since I came here." Amity trembled as she replaced the receiver and leaned against the counter for support. Goose bumps prickled her skin as she buried her face in her hands.

"Amity? Amity!" Dani cried, her soft hands on Amity's arm. "Dad! Come here. I think Amity's going to faint again!"

Amity heard heavy footsteps rush toward her and she lifted her head. "No, I'm okay, I'm not going to faint."

She allowed Clem to lead her to a bench, and her knees buckled beneath her.

"Get some water," Clem instructed Dani, "and a wet towel to put on her face."

Amity shook herself and glanced up at Clem. "Where's Titus? I have to talk to him."

"I'll go get him," Dani said. She handed her father the towel and rushed out.

Clem sat down beside Amity and patted her arm as she took the towel from him and wiped her face. "Don't worry too much, honey. I hear this often happens with women who are expecting. You'll feel better in a moment."

Amity put the towel down. "No, you don't understand. I have to talk to Titus. Someone's after me." She started trembling again. "I'm in danger."

"I'll take care of her, Clem," came a deep voice from behind them.

Amity jerked around wildly as Titus sat down beside her.

"They're after me for sure now, Titus!" she cried, reaching for him.

He took her hands and drew her to him. "How do you know? What happened?"

"F–Farris called." She took a deep breath. "They did run

her off the road, just like I thought, and now she's afraid they'll try to get me!"

"She remembers?" He took her by the shoulders and held her gently against him. "She knows for a fact that they're here?"

Amity nodded, her eyes darting nervously at the people who entered the dressing room to prepare for the play. Clem sat down on her other side.

"What's going on here, Titus?" Clem's dark gaze went from Amity to Titus.

Titus took Amity's hands in his, raising a questioning eyebrow.

She nodded.

"We should have told you weeks ago, Clem," he said.

"But I didn't want to drag anyone else into my problems," Amity explained. "I guess you're getting dragged into it anyway." She paused, taking a deep breath. "I came here to stay with Aunt Enid because someone in Oklahoma City was threatening my life." Her voice cracked and she looked beseechingly at Titus. He explained the situation to Clem, leaving out Chad's cruelty and his sister's accusations.

When Titus finished, speaking quietly and under the cover of the chattering voices around them, Clem was silent for a moment. He shook his head slowly and patted Amity on the arm. "You've been through a lot, honey. I wish there was something I could do to help."

Titus stood, drawing Amity with him. "You could call the police and alert them to the problem."

Clem stood up with them. "Of course. I'll do it immediately. And I can get someone else to take Amity's place as Salome for the night."

"Why?" Amity asked. "Nothing has changed. Now I just know for sure what I had guessed at all along. If I stay with the crowd, I'll be safe. Besides, the guards don't let unauthorized personnel backstage."

Clem shook his head. "That's no guarantee. Anyone could slip in behind them through the woods. But since you're Salome tonight, I can keep an eye on you part of the time."

The prelude music died and people filed out.

"I'll call the police." Clem left Titus and Amity and went to the phone at the counter.

Titus, with worried eyes, searched Amity's face. "Are you sure you can go through with this?"

"Positive." Amity forced a smile to her stiff lips. "Besides," she said, gesturing to the swiftly emptying room, "it's too late to back out now."

Clem rejoined them a moment later and the three of them followed the rest out. Herod and Herodias stood outside, waiting for Amity.

The tall, sandy-haired woman who played Herodias stepped toward Amity and gave her a smile. "Ready for your debut?"

With a nod, Amity moved into step with them but Titus took her by the arm and pulled her aside.

"I don't want you to let Clem out of your sight, do you understand? I don't want you alone for a moment."

"I promise."

He released her and she followed the others. As she walked beside her new companions, she heard the distant rumble of thunder. Looking up, she noted that darkness had fallen more quickly than usual. Not a zephyr stirred to ease the discomfort of the hot and heavy air. As they entered the dark set, the ever-present song of the cicadas slowly quieted until all was silent.

"Storm's brewing," Herodias remarked, looking up at the sky.

Amity followed her line of vision to the eastern horizon and saw a boiling cauldron of clouds darkening all lingering rays of light. Thunder rolled again, this time vibrating the ground.

Taking care not to disturb her heavy stage makeup, Amity

attempted to dab the perspiration from her forehead. Even the light, gauzy material of her delicate gown felt oppressive against her skin.

The giant outdoor stage lit up and the three of them, accompanied by their soldiers, walked regally through the crowded street to Herod's palace. Amity mused at the difference between the part for which she had first been selected and the character she now portrayed.

Mary Magdalene, a disciple of Christ, had followed Him and loved Him. In contrast, Salome was an infidel, the daughter of an adulteress. She had danced for the head of John the Baptist and had mocked Jesus along with her mother and uncle.

As the play progressed, Amity could not help searching the crowd of actors for an unfamiliar face, and it was a struggle to push the creeping fear from her mind. Obedient to Titus's command, she seldom allowed Clem out of her sight and she stayed close beside Herod and Herodias.

Unable to resist allowing her eyes to wander, frequently, toward Titus's bearded, beloved face, she felt secure knowing he was nearby. As often as not, she found his steady gaze on her.

To everyone's relief, a cooling breeze drifted down into the valley, bringing with it a light mist. The thunder traveled closer, but Amity still saw no lightning in the sky. The breeze gradually picked up velocity, not only cooling, but chilling the air.

As the mob in the street yelled, "Crucify him! Crucify him!" the thunder echoed against the buildings and hills and the sky danced with streaking flashes of light. Goose bumps prickled the fine hairs on Amity's arms and neck. How like this the real crucifixion must have been, as even nature had violently protested the death of the Son of God.

Lightning fairly brightened the sky to daylight as the mob shoved Jesus to the ground. One brilliant flash startled Amity and she jumped with reaction, catching her arm on the corner of a railing and cutting a gash in her skin.

She grabbed her arm, wincing at the pain, and Nelson, standing nearby, noticed the movement. He waited until the soldiers laid the cross on Christ's shoulders, then stepped across to Amity as the others led Jesus up the Via Dolorosa.

"Hurry, get backstage and get something on that," he whispered as he moved to follow the others away. "That railing was rusty. It could be dangerous, especially in your condition."

Amity stepped backstage and looked around for the others. She was alone. Where had Herod and Herodias gone? Not having played this part before, she had no idea where they usually went at this time. Titus had another scene coming up so she could not drag him downstairs with her. And she must wash this cut quickly. Nelson was right; it was risky to wait.

She took a deep, steadying breath and picked her way silently through the labyrinth of passages, all now familiar. Surely Chad's killers would not be lurking here, waiting for her to come through. And someone would probably be in the dressing room when she got there.

She stepped out onto the via and a deafening clap of thunder jerked her to a stop—the via was empty and a stealthy shadow came flitting through the darkness.

Amity froze. Who could it be? Just as the flitting form emerged, Amity took a step backward into the shadows. Then she slumped with a rush of relief when she saw Darla's shock of bright red hair flashing in the lightning. Amity stepped out into the light.

"What are you skulking around up here for?" Darla greeted. "Come and see the last part with me. The thunder and lightning will make it perfect." In the distance they could hear the pounding of nails, the shouts and cries of the people.

Amity bit her lip. She had only a little way to go to the dressing room and felt no need to spoil Darla's night so she said, "You go on; I'll be there in a moment."

Darla shrugged. "Okay, but hurry. You might miss it."

Amity watched as Darla disappeared around a curve in the

via and, once more she shivered with fear. The place was deserted and still, except for the crashing thunder and the first big splashes of rain.

Amity slipped quickly down the via and through the gate to her dressing room. Darkness enveloped her as wind licked at the folds of material around her body and whipped her hair across her face. She squinted, searching through the gloom for the stairway.

Another bolt of lightning flared close by and Amity's gaze darted to a cloaked figure by the railing. The quick surge of fear dissipated when she recognized the man.

"Nelson!" She stepped toward him. "What are you doing down here? You're supposed to be up at Golgotha."

Nelson fingered his fake beard. "Not tonight. Someone else took my place. I'm just one of the street people. Apparently Titus felt I wasn't doing my job."

Amity reached for the stair railing. "Then could you walk down to the dressing room with me? As you said, I need to take care of this cut."

Nelson reached into the folds of his cloak and pulled something out as he stepped forward, blocking her way. "Did you ever notice how strict they are around here?" he asked. "Mess up one time and they single you out as a troublemaker from then on."

Amity shook her head, confused. "What are you talking about? Nelson, what's the matter with you?"

She tried to push past him, but he stood firm. As her eyes grew more accustomed to the darkness, she glanced down at what he held in his hand. Metal glinted and her breath caught in her throat. A gun! Fear knotted her stomach.

"Nelson, what are you doing?" she asked.

"Your precious Titus can't help you now, can he, Amity?" Nelson hissed, his eyes narrowing as a pleased smile crossed his face.

Amity glanced down the stairwell. A single bulb glowed

from the landing below and the light allowed her to see the gun more clearly.

"Afraid of heights?" Nelson taunted. "Think what would happen to you. . .and to the baby. . .if you fought me."

Amity froze as sheer black fright swept through her. The baby.

"Chad Edmonds's baby, isn't it, Amity? They always say, like father, like son. That is, if you say anything to the police about Chad's confession. Where is it?"

Amity fought a growing dizziness as Nelson's face wavered before her eyes. "Chad didn't give me any confession. I never even knew about it until—"

"Until Chad's sister told her," came a woman's voice from behind them in the doorway.

Amity jerked her head around. Her heart plummeted. There stood Opal with a gun in her hand.

"Opal!" she cried. "You, too?"

"Of course not!" the woman snapped impatiently as she raised her gun toward Nelson.

Amity gasped with relief, but the relief was short-lived as Nelson grabbed her from behind and jerked her against him, shoving his gun into her ribs.

"Opal? Who are you? What are you doing here?" he snarled as he edged closer to the top of the steps.

"P.G. Wilson, private investigator," Opal answered calmly. "Sorry I can't show my identification at the moment. You'll just have to take my word for it. . .and for the fact that the police have Chad's confession safely in hand. Are some of your buddies around, or did you run Farris Edmonds off the road all by yourself?" she asked.

Amity struggled in Nelson's grasp and he jerked her against him, hard. She lost her footing on the edge of the step and fell back against him.

With a shout, Nelson grabbed for the railing, dropping his gun and scrambling to keep from pitching down the steps.

Amity cried out and reached for Opal's outflung hand, barely grazing her fingers. As she groped for a better hold, she heard Nelson fall down the steep wooden steps, his cries of pain stopping before he reached the bottom. As if in slow motion, she tumbled after him, only vaguely aware of Opal, grabbing at her clothes and screaming for her to hold on.

Slowed by Opal's grasping contact, Amity landed only six steps down, but the corners of those steps had stabbed with excruciating sharpness into her legs and back. Pain shot through her head and she cried out.

"Amity!" Opal shrieked, her feet clattering on the steps as she rushed down them. "Stay still! I'll call an ambulance!" She paused only long enough to touch Amity's face reassuringly, then ran swiftly on down.

Other footsteps echoed from the via and Amity, struggling against the pull of unconsciousness, realized the play was over. From somewhere below her, she heard a rasping, gurgling sound, and realized it was Nelson. She tried to pull herself away from the sharp steps that held her captive.

"What's happened? Who's this?" someone exclaimed from above her.

"It's Amity!" another voice, Dani's voice, cried. "Amity! Oh, no, Amity!"

Footfalls jarred the steps and Amity groaned. Someone bent over her, but the face was a blur.

"Someone get Titus!" Dani cried with a cracking voice. "Hurry!"

Soft hands touched Amity's face. "Say something, please!" Dani begged, sobs rising in her throat. "What happened?"

A gasp, and an exclamation of horror erupted from somewhere below. "It's Nelson! I think. . .I think he's dead!"

The wail of a siren reached Amity's swiftly clouding brain and then the sweet, beloved sound of Titus's voice rose above all else.

"Let me through to her!" Titus demanded.

Dani moved from Amity's side as others shifted to make way for Titus.

"Amity," he groaned as he knelt to take her face in his hands, "hold on, sweetheart." His voice broke. "Hold on. Everything will be okay." He took a deep, rasping breath. "Dear God, don't take her from me now."

With an effort of will, Amity focused her eyes on his face. She raised her hand and managed to touch his sleeve. He took her hand tightly in his own, kissing it tenderly. A warm wetness touched her fingers, and she saw tears shimmering in his eyes.

"Don't leave me now, Amity," he whispered. "I couldn't bear to lose you." He pressed her hand to his lips.

"I—I'm okay," she said, forcing the words from her throat, feeling tears of her own slide from her eyes into her hair. "Titus," she whispered, her face contorting with pain, "the baby. . ."

And then the mercy of darkness overtook her.

thirteen

"Amity. . ." Titus pleaded.

The first sensation to prick Amity's consciousness was the deep, comforting sound of Titus's voice, flowing over her like soothing ripples of cool water over the dry, parched sands of the shore. Other sounds came and left but his voice stayed, coaxing her mind awake.

The confusion and motion of the ambulance and attendants had long since ended, and as she lay, savoring the voice that had become so dear to her, she began, ever so gradually, to wonder where she was.

"I'm still waiting, Amity," Titus called softly. "Look at me, sweetheart. Listen to my voice."

She struggled to open her eyes and a faint light seeped up beneath her lids. With the light came pain, and she winced. She heard the splashing of water and felt the cool, rough touch of wet terry cloth against her skin. The pain receded again to a dull ache and she fluttered her eyelids open once more. Her vision focused and her heart contracted as she stared into Titus's worried, sea-green eyes.

He bent over her, his gaze hungrily searching her face. "Thank God," he whispered. He closed his eyes, then opened them again. "Welcome back to the world of the living, Amity. I was beginning to get worried."

"Where are we?" she asked, tearing her gaze from his to look around the room. The white bedding, the walls, and the antiseptic smells gave her the answer. "What happened?" She struggled to sit up and a sharp pain stabbed her head once more.

Titus pushed her gently back against her pillow. "You don't remember?"

"I–I must have fainted." The cloud that had lifted enough to give her consciousness refused to lift further. She wrinkled her forehead and drew her brows together. The pain got worse. "What did happen?"

"You're right, you fainted," he said quickly. Then he stood and walked to the door.

"Wait! Don't leave me!" she cried. "Where are you going?"

"Don't worry, sweetheart, I'll be back soon. I have to talk to the doctor. There's someone out here who's been waiting anxiously to see you. I'll be back in a minute," he called over his shoulder as he turned and disappeared into the hallway.

Amity struggled to sit up, this time more slowly. Pain once again shot through her head, and she lay back down on the pillow. She groaned with frustration and turned her back to the hallway to stare at the wall. What was going on?

She had been brought here in an ambulance, that much she knew. The shrill noise of the siren and the shouting, yelling voices of a crowd of people still reverberated in her head. She raised her arms into the air, looked at them, and froze. The skin and nails were torn and raw, and now that she saw marks, they began to throb with pain. She must have tried to catch herself when she fainted. That must have been what had happened.

Drops of water spotted the window and she realized it must be raining. Yes, that was right. It had stormed earlier. But she still could not recall the night clearly and she felt a growing frustration.

A light footfall, then a shaky voice, sounded from the threshold of her room. "Amity?"

She turned to see Dani stepping inside. The girl's soft blue eyes filled with quick tears, and she dashed across the room to Amity's bedside.

"Oh, Amity, I was so scared!" Dani cried.

Amity's heart contracted as she looked into the teenager's red-rimmed eyes and tear-streaked face.

"Shhh, it's okay now." She took one of Dani's slender hands and drew the girl closer. "As you can see, I'm still alive. I may not look too good, but you know things always look worse than they really are." She glanced hopefully toward the door. "Is. . .is my aunt here?"

"Not yet. Dad went to get her. He didn't want her to be alone when he told her about your. . .your accident."

"How long have I been here?"

"Not long. Oh, Amity, I was so afraid!"

"And now you know there was no reason for you to be," Amity replied with a smile. "Now, tell me how things are between you and Aunt Enid. Should I take cover behind the bed when she arrives? Or have you two settled your differences?"

"Don't worry, I'll be good," Dani assured her. "I meant what I said about giving Enid a chance. I realized I was just blaming her for my mother's actions, and I should have known that Enid wouldn't be like my mother. I really liked her before Dad got in the way, and I don't remember ever liking my mother. Oh, I loved her, but that's different."

Amity squeezed Dani's wrist. "That's my girl. There's just one thing to do."

"What's that?"

"Forgive and forget. Forgive your mother and forget the past."

Dani hesitated. "You want me to forgive my mother for killing my baby brother or sister?" She shook her head slowly. "I don't think I can." She glanced hesitantly at Amity. "Is your. . . ?" she began, then stopped, clamping a hand to her mouth.

"What, Dani?" Amity asked, a small thread of apprehension creeping across her skin as the girl shook her head wordlessly, avoiding her eyes. "Dani," she repeated, her voice betraying a growing fear, "tell me."

"I—I can't, Amity. I'm sorry," Dani cried, edging away from the bed. "Please don't make me say anymore. I promised I wouldn't say anything that would upset you if they would let me in."

Amity felt horror leap within her like a tangible thing, but she refrained from begging Dani. She shivered with sudden cold and pulled the covers up over her.

"Dani, what happened to me?" she asked quietly. "What kind of accident did I have? All I remember was walking toward the dressing rooms to clean a cut on my arm. How hard did I fall? Dani," she said more slowly, "my baby, is it okay?"

Dani's eyes widened as she backed toward the door. "Your baby? Amity, please. . .I really don't know."

Amity fell back against her pillow, sighed, and then put a hand out. "I'm sorry. I shouldn't be doing this to you. Could . . .could you please find Titus? I'll drag it out of him." She forced a shaky smile to her lips.

"Of course." Dani's eyes were still huge with fear. "I think he's still talking to the doctor. Will you be okay by yourself? You won't do anything stupid, like try to get out of bed or anything?"

"I'll. . .be fine," Amity said softly.

Dani dashed out of the room and down the hallway, and Amity closed her eyes, blocking out the light. Why would no one tell her anything? Had she lost the baby?

"Dear God, don't let it be," she whispered as hot tears forced their way out from beneath her tightly closed lids. Fearfully moving her hands across her abdomen, she repeated the prayer.

"Yes, he's still there," Titus said from the doorway.

Amity's eyes flew open.

He stepped up beside her and held out a tissue. "You're still pregnant."

She took the tissue and sniffed back some of the tears. "You're sure?"

"Yes." He eased his tall frame down onto the edge of her bed. Very tenderly, he placed his arm beneath her shoulders and drew her to him.

Her tears disappeared as quickly as they had come when she realized he was telling the truth. She lay contentedly against the comfortable pillow of his shoulder.

He massaged her neck and shoulders, easing the ache in her head. "The doctor doesn't think you have any broken bones, only bruises and scratches. The only way to be sure of that is X-ray, which, of course, we don't want to risk with the baby. Ultrasound, however, is perfectly safe, and it shows the baby is doing fine. You will have to stay off your feet for a few days, but that's because of the concussion, not the baby. He looks good."

Lulled into a blissful near-trance by relief and by Titus's electric touch, Amity peered up at him through half-closed lids. Her gaze traveled from the straight, dark eyebrows to the dark brown hair that fell down his neck to his shoulders.

"What do you mean 'he'?"

"Or she." His eyes filled with amusement. "I mean the baby. Speaking of which, are you trying to frighten poor Dani to death? She came running after me like a frightened bird, babbling about you losing your baby. No one had told her anything. She was just as afraid as you were."

"Is she okay now? Did you tell her the baby was safe?"

"I told her, and since Enid and Clem walked in just then, I left her to explain it to them. I was afraid you would become hysterical if I left you alone much longer." His hand trailed up her neck to her forehead and she closed her eyes.

"Did Dani tell you anything else while she was in here?" he asked.

"No."

"You still can't remember what happened?"

"No."

The steady massaging stopped and he lay her back down on her pillow. She opened her eyes to find him gazing thoughtfully out the window.

"What is it, Titus? What else happened that you haven't told me?"

He took her hand and raised it to his lips to kiss each grazed fingertip. "Do you remember meeting Nelson Bertrum in the stairway?"

She stared at him blankly. "I remember him telling me to hurry to the dressing room to see about my cut because the railing was rusty."

The headlights of a passing car flashed against the windowpane. Amity shut her eyes, and saw lightning flashing across Nelson's leering face.

Her eyes flew open and she gasped."Yes! He was waiting for me! He wanted to kill me!" Her whole body trembled.

"I know," Titus said quietly, his hand tightening on hers. "It's okay now. He's gone."

"He was waiting for me by the Via Dolorosa," she continued, remembering it all now with frightening clarity. "He was in Chad's ring. He helped kill Chad." She frowned and shook her head. "But what about Opal? She was there tonight. She tried to help me. What was she doing there?"

"Apparently, Farris's Uncle Jim had hired Opal to check you out. From the beginning Farris was sure you were involved in the ring. Of course, you know that. She believed that if she could get proof against you, she would get your part of Chad's inheritance."

"That's still a weak reason to keep Chad's confession from the police," Amity said.

"That wasn't the only reason. Chad and Jim had bad blood between them, and Chad knew something about Jim that Jim didn't want known. During the inheritance squabble over Chad's parents' estate, Farris sided with Jim against Chad and Chad told his extortion group about Jim's secret."

"Which was?"

"Twenty years ago, when Jim set Chad and Farris's father up in a trucking business, he sold him ten rebuilt semitrucks with stolen parts. Chad had witnesses and proof of this and his 'friends' used that information to blackmail Jim."

"No wonder Farris and Jim suspected me. No wonder they were so antagonistic toward me."

"They've since changed their minds, especially after talking to Opal, who has been watching you. . .actually, all of us. . .for the past few weeks. She was the one who moved my radio that day in my room. Opal, or rather P.G. Wilson, was the one who recognized Nelson from some dealings her agency had had with the same group in Oklahoma City. She was watching the play tonight from a specially procured seat on the set, so she could keep a close eye on you."

"That was why she refused to stay at the lodge tonight so Aunt Enid could come to the play."

"That's right."

Amity lapsed into silence for a moment. "How did they find me?"

"Farris led them right to you. They followed her from Oklahoma City when she flew here after you. Nelson infiltrated the cast only a few days before you decided to act in the play."

"How did he know I was going to join the cast?"

"He didn't. He wanted to watch me because I was so close to you. And Nelson's name is not really Nelson Bertrum. His name is Jeff McCallester. Do you remember hearing about a couple of cast members who got into trouble for searching through the director's files? That was Jeff, who had manipulated an innocent actor into helping him find the files. Then Jeff took the Nelson alias. The real Nelson was a crowd actor who had recently left after working at the play for a few months. Using the alias gave Jeff seniority so he could ask for the Peter understudy part. This also gave him the chance to switch groups, so no one who remembered the real Nelson would guess what Jeff had done." Titus shook his head. "If only I had known."

"It's over," Amity said. "Nelson, I mean Jeff is dead, isn't he?"

"Yes."

"When Opal came, he jerked me against him, and I lost my balance. I heard him falling down the stairs, and Opal tried to catch me, but I couldn't reach her well enough to get a good hold." She glanced at the rain pelting the window. "I didn't wish for his death and I never wished for Chad's death, but I've suddenly realized that I never forgave Chad for the way he treated me. Here I've been preaching forgiveness to Dani, but I've never practiced it myself. What kind of a Christian am I?"

Titus gathered her into his arms and drew her close against him. His lips caressed the soft skin of her cheek, and his beard tickled her neck. "You're a human Christian, sweetheart, just like all the rest of us." His arms tightened around her. "God loves you all the same, and so do I, Amity. . .so do I."

❧

Two days later, Doctor O'Toole released Amity from the hospital and for the first time in months she was not afraid to venture out alone. As the days and weeks passed, the nightmare receded even more, until, the day of her wedding, it was only a vague memory.

The dew-covered green grass and trees surrounding Amity glittered with the sheen of finely cut crystal. Even in the calm, mirror-smooth lake, the green reflected back at her, dazzling her with its brightness and beauty.

She stepped onto the little wooden bridge and leaned over the stout railing to gaze at her clear reflection in the water. Hers was not the traditional dress of white for a new bride, but a green that matched her eyes and revealed her love for all growing things, especially the tiny baby she nurtured in her womb.

Her gaze left the lake and traveled out across the valley, still misty from the damp night. Just there, she thought to herself, against that backdrop of trees, would be their home. She turned and looked at the church. And over there, just behind the chapel, should be the boardinghouse and school buildings.

Her ears detected the sound of another car arriving. She turned to watch as Dani and Enid climbed out of Clem's truck and walked arm in arm toward the little church. Had it only been a few weeks ago that Dani would not bring herself to speak to Enid? And now look at them.

Amity's mother and father walked out of the front doorway of the church building. She caught their attention and waved at them.

Her smiling gaze did not waver as another figure detached itself from the small group of people and walked down the hill toward her. Her heart leaped as her gaze followed Titus's large, lean frame, and she smiled a welcome as he stepped up onto the bridge to walk slowly toward her, his footsteps echoing across the water.

"It's too late for you to back out now," he said, running his hand across his smoothly shaved face, "but what do you think?"

Her gaze took in the firm line of his jaw, the determined, outjutted chin, then traveled to his mouth and stopped. A gentle flush crept up her face beneath his amused scrutiny.

She looked up, meeting his eyes shyly. "I think. . .I think I love you," she whispered. Her heart beat wildly as he closed the distance between them.

"Come now, Amity," he murmured as he drew her into his arms and lowered his mouth to hers. "Even I can do better than that."

A Letter To Our Readers

Dear Reader:

In order that we might better contribute to your reading enjoyment, we would appreciate your taking a few minutes to respond to the following questions. When completed, please return to the following:

Rebecca Germany, Managing Editor
Heartsong Presents
PO Box 719
Uhrichsville, Ohio 44683

1. Did you enjoy reading *The Healing Promise?*
   ❑ Very much. I would like to see more books
      by this author!
   ❑ Moderately
      I would have enjoyed it more if _____

   _____

2. Are you a member of **Heartsong Presents?** ❑ Yes ❑ No
   If no, where did you purchase this book? _____

   _____

3. What influenced your decision to purchase this
   book? (Check those that apply.)

   ❑ Cover   ❑ Back cover copy

   ❑ Title   ❑ Friends

   ❑ Publicity   ❑ Other_____

4. How would you rate, on a scale from 1 (poor) to 5
   (superior), the cover design? _____

5. On a scale from 1 (poor) to 10 (superior), please rate the following elements.

____Heroine   ____Plot

____Hero   ____Inspirational theme

____Setting   ____Secondary characters

6. What settings would you like to see covered in **Heartsong Presents** books?_____
_____
_____

7. What are some inspirational themes you would like to see treated in future books?_____
_____
_____

8. Would you be interested in reading other **Heartsong Presents** titles?   ☐ Yes   ☐ No

9. Please check your age range:
   ☐ Under 18   ☐ 18-24   ☐ 25-34
   ☐ 35-45   ☐ 46-55   ☐ Over 55

10. How many hours per week do you read? _____

Name _____

Occupation_____

Address_____

City_____ State_____ Zip _____

I Do

A Romantic Collection of Inspirational Novellas

Discover how two words, so softly spoken, create one glorious life with love's bonds unbroken. *I Do,* a collection of four all-new contemporary novellas from **Heartsong Presents** authors, will be available in May 1998. What better way to love than with this collection written especially for those who adore weddings. The book includes *Speak Now or Forever Hold Your Peace* by Veda Boyd Jones, *Once Upon a Dream* by Sally Laity, *Something Old, Something New* by Yvonne Lehman, and *Wrong Church, Wrong Wedding* by Loree Lough. These authors have practically become household names to romance readers, and this collection includes their photos and biographies. (352 pages, Paperbound, 5" x 8")

········· Presents ·········

Great Inspirational Romance at a Great Price!

Heartsong Presents books are inspirational romances in contemporary and historical settings, designed to give you an enjoyable, spirit-lifting reading experience. You can choose wonderfully written titles from some of today's best authors like Veda Boyd Jones, Yvonne Lehman, Tracie Peterson, Nancy N. Rue, and many others.

When ordering quantities less than twelve, above titles are $2.95 each.
Not all titles may be available at time of order.